THE
GHOSTS OF PARIS

A James Acton Thriller

Also by J. Robert Kennedy

James Acton Thrillers

The Protocol	*Sins of the Titanic*	*The Tomb of Genghis Khan*
Brass Monkey	*Saint Peter's Soldiers*	*The Manila Deception*
Broken Dove	*The Thirteenth Legion*	*The Fourth Bible*
The Templar's Relic	*Raging Sun*	*Embassy of the Empire*
Flags of Sin	*Wages of Sin*	*Armageddon*
The Arab Fall	*Wrath of the Gods*	*No Good Deed*
The Circle of Eight	*The Templar's Revenge*	*The Last Soviet*
The Venice Code	*The Nazi's Engineer*	*Lake of Bones*
Pompeii's Ghosts	*Atlantis Lost*	*Fatal Reunion*
Amazon Burning	*The Cylon Curse*	*The Resurrection Tablet*
The Riddle	*The Viking Deception*	*The Antarctica Incident*
Blood Relics	*Keepers of the Lost Ark*	*The Ghosts of Paris*

Special Agent Dylan Kane Thrillers

Rogue Operator	*Black Widow*	*Extraordinary Rendition*
Containment Failure	*The Agenda*	*Red Eagle*
Cold Warriors	*Retribution*	*The Messenger*
Death to America	*State Sanctioned*	*The Defector*

Templar Detective Thrillers

The Templar Detective	*The Unholy Exorcist*	*The Black Scourge*
The Parisian Adulteress	*The Code Breaker*	*The Lost Children*
The Sergeant's Secret		*The Satanic Whisper*

Kriminalinspektor Wolfgang Vogel Mysteries

The Colonel's Wife	*Sins of the Child*

Delta Force Unleashed Thrillers

Payback	*Kill Chain*	*The Cuban Incident*
Infidels	*Forgotten*	*Rampage*
The Lazarus Moment		*Inside the Wire*

Detective Shakespeare Mysteries

Depraved Difference	*Tick Tock*	*The Redeemer*

Zander Varga, Vampire Detective

The Turned

THE
GHOSTS OF PARIS

A James Acton Thriller

J. ROBERT KENNEDY

ISBN: 9781990418457

First Edition

For Her Royal Highness Queen Elizabeth II.

May she rest in peace.

THE
GHOSTS OF PARIS

A James Acton Thriller

"You may choose to look the other way but you can never say again that you did not know."

William Wilberforce, British politician and abolitionist

"Human trafficking is an open wound on the body of contemporary society, a scourge upon the body of Christ. It is a crime against humanity."

Pope Francis

PREFACE

The latest global estimates for modern human slavery now stands at almost fifty million people as of this writing, an increase of ten million since the last update in 2017. One in four are children, and 54% are female.

The modern definition of human slavery includes forced labor, forced marriage, debt bonded labor, descent-based slavery, and child slavery/trafficking/soldiers/marriage.

One of the most insidious aspects is human trafficking, where men and women of all ages are taken and forced into prostitution, labor, marriage, and organ removal. Perpetrators can be terrorist groups like Boko Haram, and organized crime like the Triads.

But some of the most sinister are at the high end of the slavery spectrum, where the rich don't get their hands dirty, and instead bid at auction from the comfort of their own homes for innocent young men and women who have done nothing wrong but fall on hard times.

These ghosts, forgotten by society, are easy prey for the organizers of these slave auctions.

And sometimes these ghosts aren't ghosts at all.

Sometimes they are the ones we love most.

The ones we would give our lives to save.

Unknown Location

Present Day

Tommy Granger groaned as someone shook him, his head pounding. He pushed through the fog, struggling to recall what had happened, then his eyes shot wide as he remembered. They had fought back. They all had. And they had won.

Until something had taken them all down at once.

His girlfriend, Mai Trinh, was beside him, on the floor like the rest of them. A man he didn't recognize stood in front of them with a gun aimed at them. He shook their captor, passed out on the floor, with his boot. The man called the Caretaker woke, in as rough shape as the rest of them, as the new arrival tossed zip ties at them and they bound each other's wrists.

The rebellion was over.

The gunman cut the Caretaker's bindings with a knife and the man rose, rage written on his face. His partner handed him a gun and he took it, aiming it directly at Mai who had instigated everything.

3

He squeezed the trigger.

"No!" cried Tommy, diving in front of the woman he loved in a desperate attempt to save her. The bullet slammed into him like a sledgehammer, and he cried out as he spun from the impact, collapsing to the floor.

The Caretaker's partner smacked the gun down. "Are you insane? Those two are worth ten million!"

The Caretaker spat. "She's probably nine and a half of that."

Mai rolled him onto his back and he winced, the agony unbelievable, every movie he had ever seen suddenly a lie. No one got shot then continued to fight. Words were spoken around him, but they were lost to the din ringing in his ears as he weakened. The love of his life was battling to save him, and he gazed up into her beautiful eyes and asked the question his fading mind demanded.

"Am I going to die?"

She stared down at him, her tears flowing, and he knew the answer before she spoke it.

And his heart broke as he realized he would never get to marry the only woman he had ever loved.

Lavigne Estate

Paris, France

October 8, 1898

Isabelle Lavigne stared into the mirror and smiled. Her makeup was flawless, her hair perfect, and her dress divine. Tonight would be the best night of her life. She was sure of it. Jacques would be here any minute now to pick her up, then they were meeting up with friends and heading to the most exclusive party in Paris. Rumors had been swirling around her peers at the university about parties at a wealthy aristocrat's château. No one knew where it was, only that the pickup location changed each time, and everyone was transported there in blacked-out carriages. The parties were apparently lavish, with all the food and drink one could enjoy provided.

She had been skeptical when she first heard about these parties, but as more people spoke of them, and then she finally met someone who had actually attended one, she and her friends had been determined to get an invitation. Jacques Blanchet, her childhood friend and the man she intended to marry, had somehow managed to wrangle an invitation with the location of the pickup point for tonight's party.

She had already told her parents she was staying at Caroline's house and wouldn't be back until tomorrow afternoon. She intended to get tipsy, then completely inebriated, depending on how the evening went. She was determined to tell Jacques how she felt tonight, and if he was receptive, she would be demanding a kiss.

A carriage arriving in the courtyard sent her heart aflutter, and she dashed to the window, peering outside to see Jacques stepping out. God, he was handsome. He looked up and smiled at her. She waved, her heart melting. He climbed the front steps, passing out of sight, and she rushed to the mirror, taking one last look before heading out of her bedroom and into the hallway.

His voice, so light and cheery, carried up the stairs as he exchanged pleasantries with her parents. She was certain they would approve of the match, as would his parents, both families part of the upper strata of Parisian society, both from old money. She was quite sure her mother was aware of her feelings and that her father was as oblivious as Jacques.

She stopped at the top of the stairs and drew a breath, holding it for a moment as a horrific thought occurred to her. What if he didn't share her feelings? What if to him she was merely a friend? If he rejected her, what would become of their friendship? She valued it more than anything. Yet why was that? Was it because she thought there was a future there? If there wasn't, would she still feel the same, or should she move on and find someone else to create that idyllic future with she had been imagining for years?

She shook her head. No, she was certain Jacques felt the same way. He had to. There was no way a boy and a girl could be so close for so long and not have feelings develop for each other. She had them, and he had to share them.

She headed down the staircase and Jacques caught sight of her first, his jaw slackening and his eyes widening.

"Isabelle, you look stunning!"

Any doubts she might have had as to how he felt about her were washed away by his praise. Her parents turned and her mother's hand darted to her chest.

"Oh, my child, you're so beautiful."

Her father concurred. "Stunning, absolutely stunning. All eyes will be on you tonight, my dear."

She blushed, her cheeks and ears burning from the praise and the eyes all upon her. She finished descending the steps and Jacques greeted her with a courteous bow.

"And just where are you taking my daughter tonight?" asked her father.

Jacques laughed. "Well, that's the fun of it, isn't it? We don't know where we're going, though we're assured of a wonderful time."

Isabelle's mother reached out and took her hand, squeezing it. "Just be careful, my dear. Stay with Jacques until he drops you off at Caroline's. You, of course, have heard that the Joliette boy was found dead?"

Isabelle's jaw dropped. "Pierre? He's dead?"

Her mother frowned. "I'm sorry, dear. I wouldn't have mentioned it if I had known you weren't aware. Don't let it put a damper on your

7

evening. I'm sure he got himself into something he shouldn't have. He was always a troublemaker, that one."

Jacques held out his arm. "We should get going. We have to be at the pickup point in less than thirty minutes. I'll tell you everything I know about what happened to Pierre on the way."

She took his arm, still stunned with the news. Pierre was a friend. They had all grown up together, and he was not as bad as her mother made him out to be. He had begun partying younger than the rest of them, having fallen in with his older brother's crowd. Whatever he was into certainly didn't merit death.

Jacques led her out of the house and down the steps. The coachman held open the door to the carriage and she climbed inside, not saying a word. Jacques sat beside her and they were soon underway. He took her hand. "Are you all right?"

She shrugged. "Just shocked, I guess. I just spoke to him a few weeks ago. We hadn't seen each other in ages. He's the one who told me about the parties." She faced Jacques. "What happened? How did he die?"

Jacques regarded her with a frown. "Are you certain you want to know? The details are rather grim."

"Yes. I need to know. I'm sure my imagination is far worse than the reality."

Jacques sighed. "Don't be so sure of that."

Acton/Palmer Residence
St. Paul, Maryland
Present Day, Two Weeks Earlier

Something was up, that much was clear to Archaeology Professor James Acton as the young woman he thought of as a daughter, Mai Trinh, stood before them with her boyfriend, Tommy Granger, both of them grinning ear to ear.

Acton's wife, Archaeology Professor Laura Palmer, regarded them. "All right, out with it. What has the two of you so giddy?"

Mai's left hand darted out. "Tommy proposed! We're engaged!"

Laura squealed in delight as she hopped up and down before rushing forward and embracing Mai, both of them with tears rolling down their cheeks.

Acton stepped forward and shook Tommy's hand, drawing him in for a thumping hug. "Congratulations. You've done well for yourself."

Tommy beamed at Mai. "Better than I could have ever imagined. She's perfect."

9

"She is that," agreed Acton. He held out his arms toward Mai. "Hey, don't I get a hug?"

Laura finally let their Vietnamese savior go and the young woman rushed into his arms and he held her tight. "I'm so happy for you."

She sniffed. "Thank you." She pushed back slightly so she could see him and Laura, who was now hugging Tommy. "Thanks so much, both of you. It's because of you that this has happened."

Tommy eyed her in mock disappointment. "I'd like to think I had something to do with it."

Mai giggled. "Of course. What I mean is the professors have given me a life I never thought I could have. Because of that, I met you and now not only do I have a great life here in a free, safe country, but I have good friends, a wonderful fiancé"—she held up her hand—"and one hell of a rock!"

Acton's eyes bulged as he got a good look at the ring for the first time. "How in the hell did you afford that on a university salary? Dylan must be paying you one hell of a bonus every time the CIA calls you in."

Tommy chuckled. "As much as I'd like to claim credit for socking away enough to buy something like that, it's actually a family heirloom. My grandfather gave this to my grandmother, and when she heard I was planning to propose, she insisted on giving it to me. She said my grandfather would have wanted me to have it."

Laura held Mai's hand up so she could get a better look. "So, you're talking to your grandmother again?"

"Yeah. Being with Mai made me realize how important family is, so I'm trying to reestablish those connections."

"And how's that going?" asked Acton, well aware of the estrangement between the young man and his family.

"My grandmother has been receptive, and I've spoken to my mother a couple of times, but my father refuses to speak to me." Tommy's voice cracked and Laura gave him a hug. "I suppose I don't blame him. When I was arrested for hacking the Department of Defense, it destroyed his career."

"Give it time," said Laura. "News like this might be all it takes to bring you all back together." She changed the subject back to the happy side of things. "That is a beautiful ring, and judging by the size of that diamond, very valuable. Is there a story behind it?"

"Apparently, but it was like pulling teeth to get anything out of my grandmother. All she would say was that our family descended from French high society. I pressed her, but she wouldn't say anything more, just that it was something best forgotten."

Acton already wanted to know more as he stared at the ring. "Do you have any idea how much that's worth?"

Both Tommy and Mai shook their heads.

"I'm thinking six figures."

They both gasped and Laura agreed. "Definitely. We're going to have to have you meet with our insurance broker and get a separate policy on that. Don't worry about it. We'll pay for it."

Mai held out her hand, her fingers splayed, and Acton detected a little bit of fear in her eyes. "Maybe I shouldn't be wearing it."

Tommy shook his head. "No, I'm sure my grandmother knew what it was worth. She wants you to have it."

Mai stared at it wide-eyed. "It's so beautiful, and now that I know it has a history, it's even more so." Her stare darted toward Laura. "Maybe we should call that broker sooner rather than later."

Laura laughed and took Mai by the hand. "Let's go do it right now so you can stop worrying."

The two women left the room and Acton headed for the kitchen. "Beer?"

Tommy nodded and Acton retrieved two from the fridge, twisting the tops off before handing one of the brews to his guest. Tommy took a sip and Acton a swig before they sat in the ridiculously large living area of their new home, bought in part to provide a suite for their good friend, Interpol Agent Hugh Reading. He had been overwhelmed with their generous gift and had stayed with them for a couple of months while he recovered from his ordeal in Thailand, but now he was back in London, back at Interpol, and back with his son.

And the house felt a little empty.

"This story about the ring has me curious. Do you mind if I do a little digging?"

Tommy shrugged. "Go ahead. I have to admit, my grandmother's refusal to talk about it has me more than a little curious. I think Mai and I would both love to know a little more."

Acton took another drink and sighed. "There's nothing like an ice-cold beer. I'll never understand how the Brits can drink it at room temperature and find it refreshing."

Tommy shrugged. "Maybe it's not supposed to be refreshing."

Acton chuckled. "Maybe. With those new guidelines that say we're only supposed to have a few drinks a week otherwise we risk getting cancer, they might start raising the temperature."

Tommy grunted. "I think I'd rather risk the cancer."

Acton laughed. "You and me both. If we lived our lives the way the experts say we should, life wouldn't be worth living."

Laura and Mai reappeared and Acton rose, Tommy following suit. "So?"

"All set," replied Laura. "Mai and I are going to go get the ring appraised right now so that we can have the policy in place today. Do you two want to come?"

Acton shook his head. "No, I have a little research project I have to do. But Tommy, you go ahead. I have no doubt you'd rather spend time with your new fiancée rather than this old man."

Tommy shuffled, staring at his feet. "I wouldn't put it that way."

Acton roared with laughter, slapping the young man on the shoulder. "Hey, I don't blame you. If I had a beautiful woman like that, I wouldn't be hanging out here with me either."

Laura gave him a look. "Excuse me?"

Acton's eyes shot wide and he made mock chewing sounds. "These new shoes are tasty."

"Yeah, I hope they're sweet too because that's the only sugar you're getting today."

Acton walked over and gave her a hug. "Oh, you know you're the most beautiful woman in the world."

"Uh-huh." She glanced at Mai. "Should I forgive him?"

13

Mai grinned. "I'd let him suffer a little longer."

Acton gave the smirking Tommy a sympathetic look. "Be careful, young man, what you say around this one, or you'll be tasting your shoes too."

Tommy grinned. "That's why I wear Crocs. They taste like chicken."

Acton groaned and turned to Mai. "I don't know why you agreed to marry him. It can't be for his sense of humor."

Mai snuggled up against Tommy. "I hate to break it to you, but your jokes are even cornier than his."

Acton's jaw dropped in mock affront. "My jokes aren't corny."

Laura rolled her eyes. "Let's not get started on that debate. We'll be here all day while he explains why different cultures find completely different things funny."

Acton jammed his hands on his hips. "Fine. If you don't want to partake of my infinite wisdom then get the hell out of here. I've got dirt to dig up on Tommy's family."

Laura stuck her tongue out at him then led the others out of the room as their housekeeper, Rose, swept in, cleaning up behind them.

"You find me funny, don't you, Rose?"

"Hilarious, Professor."

"Did you hear that?" he yelled.

Laura responded. "I pay her extra to humor you."

Acton eyed Rose. "Is that true?"

Rose shrugged. "I'll never tell."

"That's it. I'm going to my office. Nobody in there makes fun of me."

Île de la Cité

Paris, France

October 8, 1898

Inspector Denys Leblanc of the Paris Police Prefecture surveyed the scene, his hands on his hips as his head slowly shook. His job was to investigate murders, and a city the size of Paris meant he was kept busy, but this was something entirely different. Most murders he dealt with were crimes of passion. A man kills his wife because she cheated on him, a bar patron kills another because of an argument that got out of hand, a random mugging goes bad. But this was definitely different.

His partner, Daniel Archambault, joined him from the other end of the alley. "This makes three, doesn't it?"

"Three that we've found."

Archambault eyed him. "You think there are more?"

Leblanc gestured at the corpse. "This one's been dead for weeks and we're just finding him now. How many more are out there, hidden away like this one was?"

15

Archambault kneeled beside the body, examining it carefully.

"What do you notice?"

Archambault shook his head slowly. "It's strange. I've seen a lot of bodies since I began working with you, but until this month, they've all had heads. Without a face to associate with the body, I find it hard to imagine that this was actually a person."

Leblanc agreed. "I've seen a few headless corpses in my time, but it was always because the body had been out in the elements for so long, the head had become detached and was usually found nearby. This is something completely different. Three victims, all with their heads sawed off, their bodies disposed of, their heads yet to be found."

Archambault rose and brushed off his pants. "It's obviously the same suspect, but what's he doing with the heads?"

Leblanc pursed his lips. "Some sort of ritualistic sacrifice, perhaps? Devil worship? Certainly nothing sane. We're clearly dealing with some sort of maniac. The question is, how is he getting his hands on people like this?"

Archambault stared at him, puzzled. "People like this? You mean we have an ID on him?"

Leblanc pointed at the jacket, weathered by weeks in the elements, and torn apart by vermin. "Check the crest on his breast pocket."

Archambault kneeled once again, peering at the family crest. He shook his head. "I don't recognize it, but didn't we have a missing persons report that one of the Laurent sons was missing?"

"Yes, and that's his family's crest."

Archambault cursed as he rose. "This is remarkable. Three young men, all from aristocratic families murdered within a month of each other, all with their heads sawed off. What does it mean?"

Leblanc sighed. "It means, my friend, that we won't be getting much sleep until we solve these murders."

Acton / Palmer Residence

St. Paul, Maryland

Present Day

Professor James Acton flipped the steaks on the barbecue while Laura and Mai brought out the salads they had prepared in the kitchen. Tommy handed him a fresh beer and Acton poured a little on the steaks before taking a drink. He grinned. "Secret ingredient. It doesn't quite turn them into Kobe beef, but hey, even I'm not paying those prices."

"Well, if someone with your kind of money isn't willing to pay for it, then I'm certainly never going to taste it."

Acton laughed. "Well, you could take out a personal loan and use that ring as collateral, and eat nothing but Kobe beef for quite a while."

"If it's as good as I hear, it might be worth it, but Mai would never go for it."

"I'd never go for what?" asked Mai.

"Um, nothing."

Laura eyed the two men. "Is my husband getting you in trouble, again?"

"Only if he accepts my questionable advice," replied Acton. "These steaks are ready. How much time do you need?"

"Five minutes."

"No problem. They need to rest anyway." Acton turned off the burners and removed the steaks. The next half hour was spent with Acton and Tommy enjoying their food in silence, while Laura and Mai excitedly discussed wedding plans.

Finally, Laura leaned back in her chair and patted her stomach. "That steak was phenomenal, dear."

"Thanks to the secret ingredient."

Laura tilted her head toward Mai. "He thinks I don't know he pours his beer on the steaks as he cooks them."

Tommy chuckled. "Uh-oh, your secret is out."

"It's hardly a secret," said Laura. "I've seen him pour beer, wine, tequila, pretty much anything he can hold in his hand on whatever he's barbecuing."

Acton stretched and leaned back, getting comfortable. "Almost lost my eyebrows a couple of times. Had to replace the umbrella once. Why shouldn't barbecuing be an adventure?"

Laura gave him the stink-eye. "Burn this house down, mister, and we're moving into a shed."

"As long as I can still have a barbeque, I'm fine with that, though Hugh might object." He clapped his hands together. "So, are you going to tell them or am I?"

Laura waved her hand. "You tell them. This was your idea."

"Goodie!" He leaned forward. "So, I've been doing some digging on your family, Tommy."

Tommy shifted in his seat. "I get the feeling I'm not going to like this."

Acton laughed. "Oh, I wouldn't say that, but it is interesting. Your grandmother was right. You do come from Parisian high society."

Tommy's eyebrows rose. "Really? From what I've heard of my family, none of them have ever been wealthy, though I guess my grandmother's place is fairly big though not lavish."

"No, and there's a reason for that. A very good reason, but I'm not going to tell you what it is."

Tommy and Mai exchanged puzzled glances. "What do you mean?" asked Tommy.

"I mean, I want you two to figure it out for yourselves."

"I don't understand."

Laura gave Acton a look. "James, stop teasing them."

Acton groaned. "Fine. No one wants to let me have fun anymore. Our engagement gift to you is an all-expenses-paid trip to Paris. See the sights, stay in the finest hotels, eat at the finest restaurants or the best street vendors. Whatever you want, it's yours. Fly over on our jet and live the Life of Riley. But while you're there, you have to visit one site. I'm not going to tell you anything about it, except I'll have a car sent for you to take you there. After you visit that site, you call us, and if you haven't already figured it out, I'll explain its connection to your family."

Mai leaped from her chair. "You're sending us to Paris? Are you serious?"

Laura rose and embraced Mai. "I know you've always wanted to visit the Louvre, well now is your chance. Go see the Louvre, the Arc de Triomphe, The Eiffel Tower, Versailles. There's so much history there. There's no way you can be bored."

Tommy reached out and shook Acton's hand. "Thank you so much. It's incredibly generous of you."

Acton smiled. "Think nothing of it, but you do realize that your wedding gift is now going to be a Pez dispenser."

Laura laughed. "I think we can do a little bit better than that, but we want you two to go and have the time of your lives. Just one thing."

Tommy's eyes narrowed. "What's that?"

"We're going to leave James' little secret side trip until the end. We wouldn't want anything to spoil the mood."

Pickup Point
Paris, France
October 8, 1898

The horror of what Jacques had told Isabelle was forgotten the moment they arrived at the pickup point indicated on the invitation. Dozens of carriages were arriving and departing, clusters of people her age, many of whom she recognized, climbing into a row of carriages, their windows blocked by wood panels painted black. She had been looking forward to this part of the experience, yet after hearing what had happened to Pierre, it sent a chill up and down her spine.

Jacques picked up on her unease. "Are you all right?"

"Yes, I suppose so."

He took her hand. "Listen, we don't have to do this if you don't want to."

She firmly shook her head, reminding herself of why she was here today. "No, I want to do this. Let's have a good time. I'm sure it's what Pierre would have wanted."

Jacques chuckled. "Knowing Pierre, it's *exactly* what he would have wanted."

She pointed. "There's Caroline and the others." She waved and her best friend returned it, bouncing with excitement. Isabelle turned to Jacques. "Let's not tell the others about Pierre. I don't want to spoil the evening."

Jacques agreed. "You're right, of course."

They joined Caroline and her boyfriend Richard, along with Angeline and her boyfriend, Guy. Pleasantries were exchanged and it was clear no one knew what had happened to Pierre, or perhaps they did and had come to the same decision she and Jacques had.

Caroline eyed her. "Is something bothering you?"

Isabelle shook her head. "No, I guess I'm just a little nervous now that we're actually here."

Caroline clapped as she hopped up and down. "I know! Isn't it exciting?"

Jacques held open the door to one of the carriages and the friends all piled in. He closed the door, plunging them into darkness. Isabelle's pulse raced. She wasn't prepared for this. Not anymore. Not with the news of Pierre's decapitated body having been found only yesterday. A match flared beside her and she stared at the flame, her primordial desire for light consuming her. The wick of a candle glowed and as the intensity of the light grew, her heart calmed as the faces of her friends were revealed, including Jacques, sitting beside her with the candle.

He grinned at the others. "Good thing one of us planned ahead."

She took him by the arm and squeezed, leaning her head on his shoulder. "Thank God." The carriage jerked forward, startling them all, Isabelle and Caroline both squealing, the tension replaced with nervous laughter.

Richard Monet, Caroline's boyfriend and a new addition to the group, asked the question they all had. "Does anybody have any idea where we're going?"

Jacques shook his head. "No idea, but from what I've heard, it's grand. This will be a night we'll never forget."

Richard flicked Jacques' knee. "Didn't you say Pierre has been to two of these?"

Isabelle yelped and bit her knuckle hard.

Richard gave her a look. "What's wrong with you?"

Jacques glanced at her, his eyes asking her permission to reveal what they knew. She gave a slight nod then bit even harder.

"Pierre's dead."

Gasps filled the carriage as it made a turn. Caroline was the first to recover. "What do you mean he's dead? How? When? I mean, I just saw him a few weeks ago. He can't be dead. He's too young!"

Jacques held up a hand, cutting off the deluge of questions. "I know very little, but what I do know is, well, shocking. His body was found yesterday. Decapitated."

Caroline screamed as did Angeline, and Isabelle's cheeks quickly burned with tears, ruining her carefully applied makeup.

Richard wrapped an arm around Caroline. "So, he was murdered?"

Jacques eyed him. "Well, he didn't cut his own head off."

24

Richard rolled his eyes. "You know what I mean. Do they know who did it?"

"No. And from what I overheard, he's not the first to be found like this."

Isabelle's eyes shot wide as she turned to Jacques. "You didn't say anything about there being someone else."

He took her hand in his. "You were so upset by Pierre, I wasn't sure you'd want to know."

"I want to know everything."

Jacques shrugged. "Unfortunately, I don't know much. You know how my father is a patron of the police. One of the commissioners paid him a visit last night to tell him of the situation since he knew that our family is friends with Pierre's. I overheard the conversation. I'm not supposed to know what I know, so don't go repeating anything. Understood?"

Heads bobbed reluctantly and Caroline's shoulders slumped. "I don't really feel much like partying now."

Isabelle agreed. This night was not going as she had planned. Not at all. This was supposed to be the night she declared her love to Jacques, the night they were supposed to begin their lives together. But now it was all ruined.

Richard stared at them. "Now, wait a minute here. I barely knew Pierre. I think I met him once or twice years ago. And from my understanding, most of you have barely had any interaction with him for years. He's dead in the most gruesome manner, there's no denying that, but so is someone else. Chances are he's the victim of some madman, the killing merely random. Let's let the police worry about this and enjoy the evening that we've all been looking forward to for so long. Pierre liked to party, probably more so than anyone we know, so I say, we honor him and party like it's 1899 in his memory, and mourn him tomorrow after we've all got good and drunk and are suffering from hangovers. From what I know of Pierre, it's exactly what he would want us to do."

Jacques grunted. "It's definitely what he would do if one of us had been found."

Isabelle shuddered. "Don't even suggest such a thing."

"I'm sorry, but Richard is right. We've all been looking forward to this, and I have a confession to make."

"What's that?" asked Isabelle.

He patted his pocket that held the invitation. "I got the invitation from him. He managed to secure it at the last party. He wouldn't want it to go to waste." Jacques looked at the others. "So, are we in agreement? We're going to party tonight as if Pierre was with us?"

Richard squeezed Caroline's shoulders. "Let's make a pact right now. The six of us stick together all night and we'll all watch out for each other. If it looks like any of us are going to lose their heads, we can stop the other from embarrassing themselves." Groans filled the carriage and Richard looked at them. "What? Too soon?"

Paris Métro

Paris, France

Present Day

Tommy sat on the subway, or as they called it in Paris, the *Métro*, with Mai at his side. Their vacation had been a whirlwind so far and it showed no signs of slowing. They had hit all the major tourist attractions in the first few days, and now were merely enjoying the city and the life it had to offer, taking public transit instead of using the Mercedes rental provided by the professors. That was more used in the evenings or when they would go out for dinner to a nice restaurant, a long list of which were provided by Laura's travel agent Mary, who could get them reservations at any one of them with only a few hours' notice, including the most exclusive in town.

Today, however, had been street vendors and street clothes, the plan now to return to the hotel for some nooky and a nap.

It was the perfect trip.

A woman around their age sat across from them. "C'est beau, ça," said the woman, gesturing at Mai's ring.

Mai, who spoke fluent French, smiled and held it up, saying something in return that Tommy didn't understand, though they had agreed she would pass it off as costume jewelry if anyone asked. This appeared to satisfy the woman.

"Touriste?"

Mai nodded.

"Américain?"

Mai nodded again then the woman switched to English. "Would you two like to come to a party?"

Tommy smiled politely but shook his head. "No, thanks."

The woman put on a pout. "Why do you say no so quickly? I guarantee you'll have a good time. It's a party like no other." She reached into her purse and pulled out a flyer, handing it over. "Have you heard of the catacombs?"

They both nodded and the woman smiled.

"Of course you've heard of them, you're sophisticated Americans. It's a rave in the catacombs. Invitation only. It will be unlike anything you'll ever experience in your life, I guarantee you. There'll be music, dancing, alcohol, drugs, anything and everything you can imagine." She fished a marker out of her purse and took back the flyer, writing on the back. She handed it to Tommy. "My name is Bridgette. That's my cellphone number. Call me if you change your mind. They only have these parties every couple of months, so you're in luck. Almost nobody knows about them. If you want a vacation to remember, then I guarantee you, this is how to do it. Just make sure you bring the flyer with you. That's your invitation."

The subway slowed at the next stop and Bridgette rose, flashing a smile at them. "I hope I'll see you tonight. The fun starts at midnight." She stepped off the train and Tommy glanced at the flyer, professionally printed.

"What do you think?" he asked Mai.

She shrugged. "I don't know. What do *you* think?"

"I think it sounds kind of sketchy, but I have heard of these raves in the catacombs. It would be something to see."

"I've never been to a rave before."

Tommy eyed her. "No?"

She gave him a look. "It's not exactly the type of thing that happens in communist Vietnam."

He chuckled. "No, I suppose not. I've been to a couple of raves before I met you. They can be a lot of fun. You just have to watch your drinks, make sure nobody spikes them."

"It might be fun to let off some steam," said Mai. "Everything's been great here, but we haven't done anything really fun, anything really our age. If we were to show people pictures, you could substitute Jim and Laura for us and no one would know the difference."

Tommy laughed. "That's true for sure, though it has been a good time."

She gave him a kiss. "The best, and I wouldn't change a thing."

"But you want to go wild?"

She grinned. "Just one night. To be able to say we partied in the catacombs underneath Paris, that would be an amazing story to tell our kids."

Tommy pressed his forehead against hers. "We'll tell our grandkids. There's no way I want our kids trying to out-party us."

She giggled. "I can't believe we're going to have kids one day. I still feel like a kid."

He wrapped an arm around her shoulders. "Trust me, I feel the same way. Then it's settled, we're going to do this?"

She gave a firm nod. "Let's go wild one last time before we become old fuddy-duddies."

He squeezed her hand. "Tonight's going to be legend—wait for it!"

Paris Morgue

Quai de l'Archevêché, Île de la Cité

Paris, France

October 8, 1898

Inspector Leblanc stared at the body of Andre Lyon, nineteen years old, a young man barely in the prime of his life, a life snuffed out by a madman. Three young men, all sons of Paris' elite, each reported missing two weeks apart.

Archambault gestured toward a calendar on the wall. "You do realize that it's two weeks since this one was reported missing. If our killer keeps to his schedule, another one dies tonight."

"Yes, I can do the math. Tomorrow we'll start interviewing the friends and family of Joliette and Lyon. There has to be some connection here. There's no way three young men, all from powerful families, fall victim to the same killer unless they were targeted. We know what they have in common through social status, but was there something more? And how were they targeted? One being caught in the wrong part of

31

town I could see, but not three and not spaced so perfectly apart. I'm betting that all three of these young men were willingly with their killer."

Archambault eyed him. "You mean some sort of sexual perversion?"

"Perhaps, though I doubt on the part of the victims. I find it hard to believe that three members of high society were into such things, though anything is possible, I suppose, the way youth are these days."

Archambault, who wasn't much older than their victims, grunted. "I fear for the next century, when my generation takes over. I consider myself fairly level-headed, but you wouldn't believe some of the nonsense that comes out of the mouths of my peers."

Leblanc chuckled. "If your generation were put in charge today, yes, I agree there'd be chaos. But you've got another twenty years of experience to gain which will help tame the foolishness and save us all in the twentieth century."

The coroner, François Cartier, entered the morgue. "Oh, Inspector, I didn't realize you were here. I would have delayed my dinner."

Archambault grimaced and nodded at the corpse. "You can eat after seeing something like that?"

Cartier shrugged. "If that were all it took to spoil my appetite, I'd never eat." He smacked his rotund stomach and laughed. "Clearly, I don't have a problem."

Leblanc snickered, patting his own protruding stomach, though he had nothing on Cartier. "We could all stand to lose a few." He jerked a thumb at his young partner. "Except for the youngster."

Cartier regarded Archambault's slim figure. "Give it time. Once he gets married and stops trying to impress the ladies, he'll start to relax and enjoy an extra meal or two."

Archambault grinned. "Only if she's a good cook."

Cartier roared with laughter. "That's where you have to be careful. Mine's an exceptional cook, as you can see." He gestured toward the body. "Any questions?"

Leblanc pointed at the neck. "I assume they were all killed in the same manner?"

"If you mean they were all decapitated in the same manner, then yes. It appears the same method, and quite possibly the same blade, was used to saw the heads off all three, but that's not how they died."

"Oh?"

"I found an injection mark in this last one, in the neck." Cartier handed a magnifying glass to Leblanc and pointed at what was left of the neck. Leblanc leaned in and peered through the lens at a small puncture.

"And this wasn't on the other victims?"

"No. I'm guessing that they were drugged or killed in the same way, however the puncture mark was higher on the neckline, so removed with the decapitation. In this case, it was lower, almost at the base of the neck."

"Do we know what they were injected with?"

Cartier shook his head. "No. It could be any number of things, but the fact I found no other signs of trauma to the body suggests either the injection killed them or they were killed by head trauma. That, we of course, won't be able to confirm until you recover the heads."

Archambault took the magnifying glass and looked for himself. "And we're sure this was done before he was killed?"

Cartier shrugged. "There wouldn't be much point in doing it after, now, would there?"

"You're assuming something injected. Maybe something was extracted?"

Cartier pursed his lips. "It's possible, though I doubt it. The trauma around the hole suggests the needle was jabbed and the plunger pressed hard while the victim was alive. I think you'll find that whatever your killer is injecting them with either incapacitates or kills them quickly so that he can take his time to do whatever it is he wants to do."

"And is there any way of telling how long it was between the injection and the decapitation?"

"No, though I suspect it wasn't long. The trauma shows some post-mortem bruising that can only occur for a short period after death. There is something else I noticed, however. Help me roll him."

Leblanc gestured at Archambault, who stared at him incredulously. "There's no way in hell I'm touching that thing."

Cartier rolled his eyes then shoved a hand underneath the deceased's right shoulder, giving him a push. The body lifted off the table with a sickening squishing sound. Cartier pointed at the base of the neck. "See those two marks?"

Leblanc leaned in then held out his hand toward Archambault who returned the magnifying glass. "What am I looking at?"

"I'm not sure, but I never noticed them on the first body because it was far too decomposed, and I missed it on the second, but I reviewed the photographs and found the same marks."

Leblanc stood back up and handed the magnifying glass to Archambault who made his own examination. Leblanc scratched his chin. "Could it be some sort of clamp used to hold the neck in place while he sawed their heads off?"

"That's definitely possible, though I wouldn't think it would be necessary. A hand planted firmly on the chest or back while sawing would provide more than enough stability."

Leblanc eyed Cartier. "You sound like you've done this before."

Cartier grinned. "Only in the name of science, I assure you."

"So, if it wasn't used to hold them in place while he decapitated them, what could it be for?"

Cartier shook his head. "I have no idea, but something tells me it will all make sense once you find where he's doing this."

The Catacombs Rave

Paris, France

Present Day

Legendary isn't exactly how Mai would have described the start of the evening. When they had returned to the hotel, they had stuck to their plans and had a nice dinner since they had been told the rave didn't start until midnight. Tommy had done his due diligence, Googling the crap out of the thing, trying to find any reference to what they might be getting themselves into. He found no serious red flags. Raves in the catacombs were almost always illegal, though the articles he found indicated only the organizers were ever charged, the partiers simply rounded up and sent on their way.

He had called Bridgette to confirm they were coming and the woman had been thrilled, texting instructions on how to get to the party with a promise to meet them on the street above.

And that was where things had gone slightly awry, though Mai wasn't sure why she was surprised by it.

Bridgette had hugged them both when they arrived. "I'm so happy to see you! Do you have the invitation?"

Tommy handed it over.

"Come, let's go! The others are waiting. The party has already begun."

Tommy checked his watch. "But I thought you said it started at midnight?"

Bridgette laughed, patting him on the chest. "Oh, mon petit. I said the fun *starts* at midnight, and the fun doesn't start until *we* arrive." She led them down an alleyway as filthy as any one would find in any large city. Bridgette waved, exchanging pleasantries with two young men who then pulled on ropes, sliding a manhole cover out of the way. "Follow me." She handed the invitation to one of the men then lowered herself into the hole as Mai's heart raced.

This was really sketchy. If something were to go wrong, how would they ever escape? She wanted to turn around, to say no, but she didn't want to disappoint Tommy, who still seemed excited by everything. She took a deep breath and held it as she climbed into the hole, her foot finding a rung of the ladder. She exhaled then breathed in again, immediately regretting using her nose. The stench was terrible. She dropped deeper and saw Tommy climbing in above her.

"My, what an incredible smell you've discovered," he muttered.

"Don't worry," called Bridgette from below. "That's just here. Once we're in the catacombs, it smells normal."

"I'll take your word for it."

Mai reached the bottom and turned to see what awaited them. Tealight candles lit the way to their right, positioned on a ledge barely wide enough to walk on.

"Come this way. It's not far."

Mai waited for Tommy to step down then took his hand as they slithered along the side of the storm drain they were in, the water flowing by slowly only inches away. Terror of falling into the rank water had her taking every step carefully. They rounded a bend and the tea-lights ended just ahead.

"We're almost there," said Bridgette, pointing to a door ahead.

Mai said nothing when she noticed the lock had been broken. As she thought about it, she wasn't surprised at that fact, considering this rave was illegal. What surprised her was that she was taking part. She had never done anything illegal in her life, though that wasn't exactly true depending on one's definition of illegal. What she had done in Vietnam to help the professors was a crime in her country, but it was the right thing to do, and she didn't believe it should be considered illegal. But this definitely was. This was clearly trespassing and she was doing it in a foreign country. This was foolish and she should turn around.

Bridgette urged her forward and she found herself obeying, the driving beat of the music just ahead getting louder with each step.

"Look at the walls," hissed Tommy behind her, and she finally took a moment to look up from her feet. She gasped as a skull screamed at her. She jerked back, her jaw dropping as she realized there were scores of skulls all around her, embedded in the walls.

Tommy's arms enveloped her. "Are you okay?"

She nodded then giggled. "Yes. It just surprised me."

Bridgette grinned. "I nearly peed myself the first time I saw it. You hear about it, you see the pictures, but it's quite a different thing to actually see the real deal."

Mai had to agree. "It's incredible." She reached out and touched one of the skulls. Her hand jerked back as she remembered what she was doing.

"Unbelievable," muttered Tommy. "I can't believe this is how they used to bury their dead."

Bridgette took Mai by the hand. "Let's go! If you think this is amazing, you ain't seen nothing yet, as you Americans like to say." They followed her down the passageway lined with stone and skulls, toward the blaring music, so loud it vibrated through her entire body, the experience almost erotic. They emerged into a large chamber, packed shoulder to shoulder with flesh. Well over one hundred, if not two hundred people their age writhed to the music, gyrating against each other in an orgy of anonymity.

It was terrifying.

It was thrilling.

Bridgette led them deeper into the crowd, grabbing three drinks off a tray held high by someone. She handed them each one then downed her own. "Let's party!"

Mai glanced at Tommy who shrugged then downed his own drink. Mai followed suit as Bridgette turned, dancing seductively, rubbing her body against Mai's. Mai had never danced like this, not with a woman, and she glanced over her shoulder at Tommy who was directly behind

39

her, his body pressed against hers as the crowd closed in on them. She turned around to face him and let herself go, rubbing her body into his as Bridgette ground into her from behind. It was the most erotic experience of her life, and it had her heart hammering, her body aching to be taken.

She grabbed Tommy's head, pulled him closer, and kissed him. Bridgette's lips pressed against Mai's cheek, her tongue flicking out at Mai's neck as she reached past her, grabbing Tommy by the waist and pulling them in tighter. Tommy's arms reached around, gripping Bridgette, the two of them squeezing Mai between them.

And she loved it.

The music continued to pound as her entire body melted. A drink was shoved up to her face and she turned her head and opened her mouth, the contents poured down her throat, not caring what was in it, just hoping it would contribute to the overall experience. Tommy did the same as did Bridgette behind her. He kissed her again and she kissed him back as if they were in the throes of passion, the fact they were surrounded by hundreds of people lost on her.

And as the drinks took effect, her inhibitions lowered even more, and rather than being shocked, she found herself thrilled that Bridgette had repositioned herself so that the three of them were now kissing. What should have made her jealous instead turned her on feverishly, and she had no doubt this would be a night they would never forget for as long as they lived.

And they were definitely not telling their children or grandchildren about it.

Rave Control Center

Paris, France

"Do you have eyes on Bridgette?"

Victor pointed at camera number two. "Yes, she's got two live ones by the looks of it."

"The American tourists?"

"Yes. The girl though looks Asian, maybe Vietnamese."

"That's not a problem. Get some good video of that, then put it up on the marketplace. That's some of the hottest shit I've ever seen."

Victor had to agree as he adjusted himself. He pulled up the footage on a separate screen, zooming in on the three lovers, then posted it on the marketplace with a note that Bridgette wasn't included in the auction and that the other two were American. Bids immediately poured in for both of them, though the Asian American girl's numbers climbed far faster than the Caucasian male, yet his numbers were impressive as well. There was an appetite out there for young White men, especially among the Saudi crowd.

"How's it looking?"

Victor glanced over his shoulder at the Operator, a man whose name he didn't know. "She's going to bring in some big numbers. He's looking pretty good too. As soon as I put up that they're both American, the numbers went through the roof. Usually, we only have French on offer."

"Yeah, they do like their Americans, don't they?"

One of the other controllers sitting next to them laughed. "I just got a million-dollar offer on Bridgette."

The Operator chuckled. "If she wasn't so good at bringing in high-value targets, I'd accept it." He pointed at the screen. "But look at what she's fetched us tonight."

Victor glanced at the numbers, his eyebrows shooting up. The American girl was up over two million already, her partner at over half a million. He shook his head in awe at the money involved here.

He'd been a ghost for two years before he had been brought into the operation. He had run away from home and had been living on the streets when he had met Bridgette's predecessor. She had found out he had a knack for computers and he had been brought into an operation that paid him more than he could have ever imagined, but came with a price—once you are in, you never left.

Unfortunately, by the time you were told that, you were already in. But he didn't mind. He loved the work, and it meant he would never be a ghost again. At first, he had felt bad about what he was doing. The lives of those chosen were over, futures they had looked forward to replaced with a horrifying life as a slave, bought and sold by the rich, ferried around the world like cargo.

But it wasn't his fault. If he wasn't doing the work, someone else would, so why should he still suffer on the streets and let some other lost soul live the life he now lived? What he was doing was wrong, but he had been forced into it. And it wasn't by the Operator or his bosses. It was by his parents, his father especially, who had abused him for years. It was why a lot of the ghosts were on the street, the stories of sexual abuse rampant. Parents, teachers, and those supposed to listen. For him, it had been his father, for Bridgette it had been her stepbrother.

His console beeped and his jaw dropped as he pointed at the screen. "Ten-million-dollar final offer for both!"

"What are the individual bids up to now?"

"Three and a half for her, seven-fifty for him."

"Take it."

Victor hit the button, locking in the bid, and sealing the fate of the two Americans.

The Catacombs Rave

Paris, France

Tommy couldn't believe what was happening. A sexual fantasy was playing out that he never imagined could happen to him, and Mai was giving every indication she was up for it. He would have expected to be terrified at the notion of having to sexually satisfy two women, let alone one, but for some reason he was completely into it. As Mai ground her hips into his, kissing him passionately, Bridgette's hands explored his body as he explored hers.

This was definitely going to be a night he never forgot.

Bridgette grabbed two more drinks from somebody passing by and held one up to his lips, the other to Mai's, and they downed them. He was already feeling it, a lot harder than he would have expected, but he didn't care.

This was the greatest night of his life.

Bridgette pushed Mai down by the shoulders and Tommy groaned as his fiancée fumbled with his zipper. Bridgette grabbed Tommy and kissed him, the thrill threatening to explode his heart. He opened his closed eyes to see if anyone else was paying them any attention but found he could barely focus, everything a blur.

A moment of panic shot enough adrenaline into his system to help him briefly focus. Something was wrong. Three drinks shouldn't be blurring his vision, and Mai should definitely not be doing what she was about to do in public, no matter how caught up in the situation they both might be.

He pushed back from Bridgette and reached down, hauling Mai to her feet, and was shocked when she could barely stand.

"What's wrong, mon chéri? Don't you like to have fun?"

He stumbled back from Bridgette, holding Mai against him. "What was in those drinks?"

"Just something to loosen you up. Nothing to worry about." Bridgette took him by the hand. "Come with me. I'll get you some water."

Water sounded like a good idea, so he allowed himself to be dragged through the crowd as he held Mai tight, his fiancée completely out of it. They had been drugged, with what, he didn't know, but as he squinted at those around him, some of the partygoers briefly coming into focus, he was quite certain they weren't the only ones. Half of those he could make out were in some state of undress, with countless sexual acts underway.

He had been so caught up in his own situation he hadn't noticed what was happening around him the entire time. A pain behind his eyes caused him to squeeze them shut as a piercing sound filled his head. He struggled to control his breathing as panic set in and Bridgette continued to tug him to the wall opposite where they had entered.

He fought hard to focus and failed. Was this just a party gone bad, or was something more going on here? Everyone seemed to be having a good time, too good a time, but no different than he and Mai. Was this just an experience he should let himself enjoy, and tomorrow they would wake up and it would all be over, or was this something he should get them out of?

Bridgette led them into another passageway and he propped Mai up against the wall, her head lolling to the side, the third drink having overwhelmed her. Even if this were innocent, there was no way he could let this continue. Anything she might do, she couldn't possibly consent to, and his sexual fantasies never included taking advantage of a woman in this state, especially a woman he loved. Bridgette walked away, deeper into the passageway, then returned a few moments later with three bottles of water.

"Your girlfriend doesn't have a very high tolerance for fun, does she?"

"What do you expect? You drugged her." Tommy's words were slurred despite his best efforts. "You drugged *us*."

"Just to have a little fun." Bridgette wrapped her arms around his neck and kissed him. "Nothing says we can't have a little fun while she sobers up." Her fingers ran through his hair then one hand dropped, reaching into his unzipped fly and he groaned, Mai momentarily forgotten against the wall. He couldn't believe how he was reacting. It was so out of character for him.

He pushed away. "No, this isn't right, something's wrong."

"Good night, my darling."

He stared at Bridgette, puzzled, then collapsed, his world fading to black as the driving rhythm continued to pound behind him.

The Party
Unknown Location
Paris, France
October 8, 1898

The door opened to the carriage and light poured in. Isabelle blinked several times to adjust her eyes from the dim light of the candle. A footman held out a hand and she took it as he helped her down onto the cobblestone of what turned out to be a large, walled-in courtyard.

It was well lit, and for a moment, she forgot all about Pierre. She stared up at the château, tastefully lit, highlighting all its architectural features. It was in excellent condition, and it was clear whoever lived here came from money.

Jacques took her arm as ushers guided them inside, the latest ragtime hit from America's Tin Pan Alley playing over a gramophone so loud, she wondered how it was even possible. And as they walked through the massive doors and into the largest ballroom she had ever seen in a home, a smile spread.

Hundreds of the youth of Paris' elite were milling about, some dancing, all with drinks in their hands. Waiters with hors d'oeuvres and drinks made their way through the revelers, their trays picked clean by the time they completed their circuit.

It was spectacular.

She turned to Jacques. "Isn't this fantastic?"

His smile was as big as hers. "Isn't it? This is more than I imagined!"

A waiter walked up to them with a tray of champagne flutes and they each took one. Glasses were clinked, toasts were made, and as the evening progressed, the best night of Isabelle's life unfolded. It wasn't long before she was feeling no fear, and she was ready to initiate her plan.

But first, things had to be perfect.

She and the girls made it into one of the bathrooms. The lineup had been long, and by the time she got in she was dancing to keep herself from having an accident. But now she was relieved, and they were all touching up their makeup in front of the crowded mirror. While the château no doubt had many bathrooms, most of it was cordoned off, leaving only half a dozen from what she had heard.

But that didn't concern her. Her makeup was perfect, she had a buzz going that had her comfortable in her own skin, and she was ready.

"This is it, I'm going to do it."

Caroline stared at her in the mirror as she touched up her lipstick. "You're going to do what?"

"I'm going to tell him how I feel."

Angeline's eyes narrowed. "You're going to tell who what?"

"I'm going to tell Jacques that I love him."

Both of her friends squealed, Caroline spinning around and grabbing her, giving her a hug. "I didn't know you loved him!"

Angeline batted a hand at her. "How could you not? The two of them are inseparable. They always have been."

"I know, I just assumed though that they've been friends for so long, things would never change." Caroline regarded Isabelle. "Do you think he feels the same?"

Isabelle clasped her hands in front of her chest. "Oh God, I hope so."

"He adores you," reassured Angeline. "Go tell him."

Isabelle grinned at her friends. "Wish me luck."

"Luck!" they both echoed, giggling with glee as the three of them headed out of the bathroom. They strode down the hallway toward the party, arm-in-arm, both sides lined with couples drinking and kissing. It was a night for passion. It was a night for abandonment.

It was a night for love.

The three of them marched swiftly down the hall as if they owned the place, alcohol-fueled confidence and an upbringing that taught them they were second to none parting the crowd. They came into the ballroom, finding the dancers now far outnumbered the wallflowers.

Isabelle's eyes scanned the room, searching for Jacques. "Do you see him?"

Caroline shook her head. "No." She pointed. "But there's Richard and Guy." She waved at them and they waved back, weaving through the dancers to join them.

"Have you seen Jacques?" asked Isabelle.

50

Guy glanced away, clearly uncomfortable, but Richard laughed and pointed down another hallway. "Last I saw him, he was kissing some girl down there."

Caroline swatted him and he gave her a look. "What? What did I do?"

And he was right to question it, for he was the newest member of the group and had no idea how Isabelle felt about Jacques. Isabelle squeezed her eyes shut as her pulse raced in her ears, her stomach churning at the betrayal.

Caroline took her arm. "Are you all right?"

"I can't believe he would do that! I can't believe he would do that to me!"

"I'm sure it's some kind of misunderstanding," said Guy. "He's had a lot to drink. He doesn't know what he's doing."

Isabelle's chest tightened and she pressed her palm against it as she labored to breathe. "I have to get out of here."

Guy turned. "I'll go get Jacques."

Angeline reached out and grabbed him. "Absolutely not. He can find his own way home after what he's done."

Guy frowned but acquiesced, and the five of them headed for the front door. Within moments, they were loaded into a carriage and plunged into pitch darkness as Jacques was the one who had brought the candle. But that was fine with her. Her life was over, her dreams shattered, and the last thing she wanted was to see the pity on her friends' faces.

Jacques was dead to her.

The Catacombs

Paris, France

Present Day

This was Victor's favorite part of the night—leftovers. The auction had been extremely successful, ten partiers sold, eight girls and two boys, a haul of almost twenty million, of which he'd get his 0.2% cut. It sounded like a pittance, but forty thousand for a night's work was well worth it, though it wasn't really a single night.

The search for the next venue would begin in the morning, then the setup usually took several days, tapping into the electrical, running the wires for the cameras, the lighting, the music. It was quite the production, and it was a party he would kill to attend himself if he didn't know the truth behind it.

It was a lure for the ghosts, for those who lived on the streets of Paris, who had no reason to live and were willing to risk everything for the chance at a good time that cost them nothing. Yet the price to pay wasn't always in money. Ten people's lives were over. They were already on their way to their new owners, the modern-day slave trade far bigger than anyone realized.

His team was responsible for hundreds over the past couple of years since he'd been involved, and he had no idea how many might have been taken before that. And that was just this operation. There were setups similar to this in every major city in the world. Women were kidnapped and sold routinely in Africa and Asia—they were easy to come by. The real prizes were white men and women, especially American and European citizens. The bids were extremely high, especially for blonde American girls. Just one could fetch the price of one hundred girls kidnapped by the likes of Boko Haram and sold into the slave trade. It's what made this operation so lucrative. He had no idea who was behind it, the only name he knew was Bridgette's. Everyone else was called by their title.

"I think that's the last of it," said one of the unnamed minions known as the Cable Guy, and Victor inspected his checklist, nodding. They left no trace behind beyond those who attended the party. Every camera, every cable, every speaker, every clip used to hold the wires, everything was accounted for.

Then there were the leftovers, the partiers who had partaken so hard they were still lying on the floor of the catacombs.

The Operator entered the chamber. "Are we good?"

"Yup. Everything has been packaged up and accounted for. We're ready to leave. Our haul?"

"Already in the transport. They'll be out of Paris within the hour. Final deliveries should all be completed before the end of the week, then you'll get your cut."

"Can't wait. I've had my eyes on a new car for months now."

This appeared to pique the Operator's interest, which suggested he was a car aficionado. "What were you thinking of getting?"

"Well, as much as I'd like to get a traditional car with a throaty engine, I'm going electric."

"Tesla?"

"No, I don't like the look of them. The Model S is nice, but it's way overdue for a redesign. There's nothing worse than buying a car then the next year they come out with the update."

"Tell me about it. I never buy a car now without looking to see what the manufacturer's schedule is for redesigns. So, if you're not getting a Tesla, then what are you getting?"

"Let's just say it's a sporty British number that I think will work well with the ladies."

The Operator laughed. "Well, you'll definitely be able to pull the old trick of claiming you're out of gas, because those things are notorious for their electrical problems, so just think what an electric version would be like. Besides, you're French. You shouldn't be driving a British car."

"What? You want me to drive a Renault?"

"No, but at least drive something from the continent. Mercedes, BMW. Hell, even a Fiat would be more reliable."

Victor pointed at a gorgeous girl lying on the floor that had somehow been missed by the bidders last night. "You think she's going to get in a Fiat with me?"

The Operator laughed. "In her state, she'd get in anything. Is that the one you want?"

"Yeah, I think she'll do nicely."

"All right then, get her out of here. I want this entire op shut down in the next five minutes."

Victor picked the girl up and slung her over his shoulder in a fireman's carry. Besides the ridiculous money, this was the best part of the job, and what he would do with this girl over the next few days would help him forget what he had participated in.

It was a horrible life from the outside, but once you were in it, it had its delights.

The Party

Unknown Location

Paris, France

October 8, 1898

Jacques laughed and pushed the unbelievably gorgeous woman away. "I'm sorry, but I can't do this."

She kissed him again then stared in his eyes, hers filled with lust like he had only dreamed of. "You say you can't, but you certainly can."

He pushed away yet again from the most erotic experience of his life. He had never kissed a girl, not more than a peck, and all had been with merely friends or relatives. There was only one girl he wanted to kiss like this, and that was Isabelle. He loved her with all his heart and was desperate to tell her how he felt but was terrified of what might happen should she not feel the same.

But this was not the way to demonstrate his love. The woman had surprised him, grabbing him away from the others and dragging him down the corridor. He had thought it was all in good fun until she had shoved him against the wall and started kissing him. He had been caught up in the moment, nothing like this ever having happened to him before in his young life, yet it had to stop, because judging from where this girl's hands were roaming, she was determined to go all the way.

And he was terrified he wasn't strong enough to resist.

He pushed back once again. "No, I can't do this."

Her hand gripped what raged below. "I think you can. I think you want to."

"Of course I want to, but there's someone else. Someone I love."

They were almost at the end of the corridor now, the fact she had been pushing him down it all along missed. "I want to show you something." She opened the door at the far end and dragged him through. She closed the door behind them then pulled a string on her bodice. She yanked at the most revealing outfit he had ever seen, exposing her large breasts. She grabbed his head and yanked it down, burying his face in her flesh and he moaned, unable to resist, the temptation simply too great.

His tongue darted out and she groaned, then he pictured Isabelle and his heart broke at how weak he was, how taken in by this virgin experience. He couldn't stop himself, it was simply too much, his senses overloading with the erotic experience. Before he knew it, he was at the bottom of a set of stairs and she was leading him into another room. The doors closed behind them with a thud then gas lanterns surrounding the room flared as she continued to squeeze him through his pants, leaving him blind to what was around him.

She kissed him again and stared into his eyes as she gripped the back of his neck. "And now you are his."

Something jabbed in the side of his neck and his eyes shot wide from the pain as terror filled his heart at the sickeningly twisted smile he now faced.

"You have done well," came a voice from behind him and he spun, his hand darting toward his neck, horrified to find something sticking out of it. But that was nothing compared to what lay in front of him—a long dining table, the chairs removed from one side, five of the chairs facing him occupied by guests with the most horrific expressions of terror he could imagine. And as he collapsed to the floor, his heartbeat slowing, his vision blurring, he finally noticed the most sickening aspect of the display.

They weren't guests at all, they were merely heads mounted to the high-back chairs.

And with his last ounce of strength, he screamed.

Acton/Palmer Residence

St. Paul, Maryland

Present Day

"James, wake up."

Acton flinched then groaned. "What time is it?"

"Just after six."

"In the morning? Are you crazy?"

"I just got an urgent call from Mary about Tommy and Mai."

This caught his attention and he bolted upright. "Okay, I'm up." He wasn't so sure about that declaration as he rubbed his eyes, but the concern on his wife's face soon had him fully alert. "What's going on?"

"I just got a call from Mary. She said that the driver sent to pick them up to go to that tour you arranged couldn't reach them."

"Maybe they changed their minds and found something better to do. Did you check our messages? Normally they send us something each morning telling us what they're up to."

"No, there was nothing from them. Mary was concerned, so she had the hotel check the room and they weren't in it, and it looks like they didn't sleep there last night."

Acton's eyes narrowed. "Maybe they stayed somewhere else. The car?"

"The rental is in the hotel's lot. As far as Mary can tell, they went out for dinner last night and came back to the hotel, then left again around eleven PM."

Acton's eyebrows shot up. "That's a little late to be going out."

Laura shrugged. "Not really. They're kids."

Acton grunted. "I'm usually asleep by eleven unless my young wife is jumping all over me."

Laura gave him a look. "I've never heard you complain." She wagged her phone. "I'm concerned."

Acton stood, heading for the bathroom. "So am I, though I'm not sure what we could do about it. I'm sure it's the same there as it is here. They're not considered missing until they've been gone for forty-eight hours, and for all we know, they went out, met some people, and stayed at their place."

"That's definitely possible, but I've sent them each several messages and both their phones are showing that they're offline."

Acton flipped up the toilet lid, releasing his morning ritual on the porcelain. "Wait a minute, Tommy's offline?"

"Yes."

"For how long?"

"It looks like since before midnight."

60

"Okay, now I'm concerned. I don't think that boy's been offline for more than three hours in his life. It's still probably nothing, but maybe we should give Hugh a call, see if he can do a little poking around."

"That's exactly what I was thinking." She dialed and put the call on speaker as it rang.

Acton continued to pee. "You couldn't have waited?"

"You could have been doing number two and I'd still call."

"Reading." The answer was curt which meant their friend wasn't at home.

"Hi, Hugh, it's James and Laura."

"Oh, hi, guys. Wait a minute, isn't it six in the morning there?"

"Tell me about it," said Acton as he finished his donation to the city's water supply.

"What the hell was that?"

Acton grinned at Laura. "Blame Laura. She's the one who wouldn't let me finish my piss before she called you."

"Bloody hell. You Yanks have no couth."

"Hey, I wasn't the one who dialed. The Brit did."

"Fine. What is it that has you calling me in mid-stream so early in the morning there?"

"It's Tommy and Mai," said Laura. "We haven't been able to reach them, and nobody's seen them since last night."

"It's just a little past noon in Paris. Is there any reason to get excited so soon?"

"They missed a scheduled pick-up, and the hotel says they didn't sleep in their room last night."

Acton leaned toward the phone as he washed his hands. "And Tommy's been offline since before midnight last night."

"Huh. That *is* unusual. I'll tell you what, I'll put the feelers out. I'll check the hospitals and morgues, look for any reports of anything unusual in Paris last night. I'm sure it's nothing. They probably just went out and met up with some people and spent the night. You'll probably be hearing from them soon. They're kids on vacation. Let them have fun without Mom and Dad constantly breathing down their necks."

Acton rather liked being called a dad, even if it was in an insulting fashion. "I'm sure you're right, buddy, but take a look anyway and get back to us as soon as you can."

"Will do, but in this case, no news is good news. They're probably just out being young and dumb."

"I'm sure it's nothing," agreed Laura. "But you know me. I worry about them."

"No problem, I'm on it. Talk to you soon."

The call ended as Acton dried his hands. He regarded his wife. "Now what do you want to do?"

She stared at the floor. "I'm not sure. I guess we should just wait to hear something from Hugh."

Acton suppressed a smile. "Why don't you give Mary a call and book a flight?"

Laura bounced. "Good idea. We can always cancel it if we hear something."

"Just book it for London. We can visit Hugh if it turns out to be nothing. I'd hate for the kids to find out we ended up in Paris because they decided to have fun without getting permission from the mothership."

She flipped him the bird then dialed, leaning in and giving him a kiss. "Thank you for knowing me so well."

He headed for the bedroom. "You know where I'll be if you really want to thank me."

Unknown Location

Mai woke, her head pounding with the worst hangover she had ever experienced. She wasn't much of a drinker, a glass of wine or a bottle of beer here and there. She could count on one hand how many times she had been drunk in her life, but she only remembered two drinks and the dance floor.

Her heart raced. What had happened? She remembered dancing with Tommy, but Bridgette was there too, rubbing up against her, kissing her. She shuddered. It was completely out of character for her, and as she recalled the night in brief flashes, it revolted her. She would never do anything like that, even with a couple of stiff drinks.

Her eyes shot wide. She had been drugged. They had both been drugged. There was no way Tommy would have acted the way he did either. She squeezed her eyes shut and pinched the bridge of her nose as the pounding in her head worsened. She needed water. She rubbed her eyes. She didn't remember coming back to the hotel. Tommy must have gotten her here. The bed jerked and her heart leaped into her throat as her taxed brain finally took notice of her surroundings.

She was in what could best be described as a coffin, but as she examined it, she realized it wasn't that at all, though it did match the size she would expect a coffin to be on the inside. There were no windows, no doors, no openings whatsoever. There was a light behind her head that gently lit the compartment, but other than the fact she was on a mattress that had a fitted sheet and that she was covered in a comforter, there was nothing else of distinction in sight.

Her heart raced as she lifted the comforter and found herself naked. And it was then, over the pounding of her pulse in her ears that she sensed the vibrations. She was in a vehicle of some sort and they were moving. She cupped a hand to her ear and could barely make out anything beyond a hum.

Tires on pavement.

She had been kidnapped, that had to be what was going on here, but she had never heard of anyone being kidnapped like this. A comfortable bed, clean sheets, and a blanket? She wasn't restrained in any way, the only violation, so far, the removal of her clothes, though what had happened to her while she was passed out, drugged, she shuddered to think.

Her eyes shot wide as the fog cleared. "Tommy!" she screamed, finally realizing he wasn't there with her.

There was no reply.

"Tommy!" she yelled at the top of her lungs again, and still there was no reply. She kicked and punched at the walls surrounding her to no avail, then finally curled into a ball and sobbed. What had happened to Tommy? Had he been kidnapped too? Was he dead somewhere after trying to defend her, or was he out there searching for her? She prayed for the latter, for the longer it took for someone to start looking for her, the less likely they were to find her.

And she was terrified at what awaited her at the end of her journey.

Interpol United Kingdom Liaison Office, New Scotland Yard
London, England

Interpol Agent Hugh Reading checked his email yet again. He had put out an alert through Interpol, and so far, there had been no reply from the French authorities about anything matching Tommy and Mai. He was getting antsy.

His partner, Michelle Humphrey, tapped on the door. "Anything?"

He shook his head. "Nothing. I still think Laura is overreacting. These are two mid-twenties kids who just got engaged and they're on an all-expenses paid trip to Paris. I think they're just up to a little bit of fun."

"Well, you might just be right about that."

He eyed Michelle "What do you mean?"

She handed over her tablet. "I was browsing their social media since the professors aren't really on there so don't have access. It's amazing what Gen Zers will post. Basically every moment of their lives with everything set to public so that they can get more followers."

Reading grunted. "Well, in the boy's defense, he's actually trying to make a career out of it, so the more followers he has, the more advertising revenue he gets."

"Oh, he's one of those, is he?"

Reading shrugged. "It's a new world." He looked at the screen. "What is this?"

"A party invitation."

Reading's eyes narrowed as he zoomed in on the image then used his finger to drag it around so he could read every square inch of it. "My French is merde. Some sort of party in the catacombs?"

"Yes, it took place last night. Invitation only. You couldn't get in unless someone in your party had the printed version of what's in that photo. It was on Tommy's Insta account, posted around ten-thirty last night with a comment that said, 'Underground party in the catacombs! YOLO!'"

Reading stared at her. "YOLO?"

"You only live once."

"Oh. What's with all these acronyms? I don't understand kids today."

Humphrey shrugged "IDK."

"Huh?"

"Just kidding. Anyway, that party is where we start looking for your friends."

He regarded her for a moment. "Don't tell me you think something has happened to them now too."

"I did some checking with our Paris contacts. Those raves are illegal and they usually involve street youths. If your two clean-cut American tourists got invited to this party, they might have been targeted."

"Targeted for what? It's not like they're rich."

"They might not be rich, but if they were seen coming in and out of a five-star hotel driving a rented Mercedes, they might have been mistaken for being rich. But you're forgetting one thing that you told me a few days ago."

"What's that?"

"That girl's walking around with a ring worth well into the six figures. If somebody noticed that, that's enough to kill for."

A shiver ran up and down Reading's spine at this forgotten fact. Humphrey was right. They could absolutely have been targeted. The ring could have been spotted, an invitation to an illegal party extended, then when they were underground, they could have been mugged or even killed for what was on Mai's finger.

He ran his fingers through his hair. "All right. A ring like that isn't something to take to a pawn shop, assuming they knew what they had. Either way, even if it did end up at some pawn shop, the pawnbroker is going to know what he has and it's going to be going on the black market fast. Laura said they had it appraised so that means there are photos and specs on file. I'll contact them and have them sent over, and then I want them out on the wire to all our contacts." He rose "I think I'm overdue for a visit to Paris."

"Do you honestly think the boss is going to let you go?"

He grinned at her. "Not if *I* ask."

Acton/Palmer Residence

St. Paul, Maryland

Acton zipped up his suitcase as Laura rushed into the room. "I just had all the paperwork sent over to Hugh about the ring. Oh my God, do you think that's what this is all about? I knew I should've told her not to wear that while they were on vacation. It's one thing to wear it around here in familiar surroundings, but not in a foreign country."

"There was no way she wasn't going to wear it, no matter what we said. She was too proud of it, and it was properly insured, thanks to you. If someone wanted it, hopefully they were smart enough to just hand it over."

Laura dropped onto the bed. "If that were the case, then they would've been back at the hotel by now."

Acton shook his head. "Not necessarily. If they did go to this party like Hugh thinks they might have and got drunk, they might not have even discovered the ring was missing until they woke up wherever they happened to spend the night. Then if I were them, I would've gone to the police station to file a report."

"But why wouldn't they have called us?"

"Because maybe when the ring was stolen, so were their phones. I still think we're going to find them alive and well and just embarrassed. But I already called Mary and had her move up the flight and rebook it for Paris. Reading sent me a message while you were dealing with the insurance. He and Michelle have approval to go to Paris."

Laura's hand darted to her chest. "If Interpol thinks it's serious enough to send two agents—"

He cut her off. "No, Hugh said the only reason they got approval to go is because his boss prefers it when he's in a different country from her. He's being indulged. Now, you finish packing and let's get to the airport. Our plane will be ready in an hour and we can be in Paris by this evening, hopefully having dinner with Tommy and Mai, laughing about the whole thing."

Laura sighed. "I hope so." She paused "Do you think we should reach out to Dylan?"

"No!" Acton held up a hand, his response a little too firm. "Sorry, I mean, no, it's way too soon for that. The sad thing about this is that the person I would reach out to in a situation like this would be Tommy. For now, let's just get over there and let Hugh do his job. I'm sure if anyone can get to the bottom of this, it's him."

Unknown Location

Tommy groaned, his head pounding as if he had polished off two bottles of JD, or at least that's how he imagined how bad it would be. He couldn't stand hard liquor. Beer was his thing, wine if it was a formal dinner, though Acton was introducing him to the joys of port, and scotch had been the beverage of choice at celebrations after an assignment at Dylan Kane's secret operations center. But whatever he had drunk last night had KO'd his brain into the next zip code.

He remained lying down, his eyes closed as he forced his way through the fog, struggling to recall what had happened last night. They had gone to a party in the catacombs. That one memory triggered a flood. Bridgette, the dance floor, the drinks, the kissing, the drugs, the passing out, Mai nearly unconscious.

"Mai!" He bolted upright, his head smacking against something, and he fell back onto the bed, grabbing at his new source of misery. He forced his dry eyes open and peered about, panic setting in. He was in some sort of box. It almost reminded him of the Japanese pod hotels he had seen on TV, though all he could see were the walls that surrounded him, the bed he was lying on, and the light behind his head.

There were no amenities.

Bridgette had kissed him after they had left the party and he had passed out within moments. He licked his lips and there was an odd aftertaste, pungent, acidic-like. He had read once about hookers applying a drug to their lips so that when they kissed their client, he would pass out then they could rob him with ease.

That had to be what happened to him, but where the hell was he? What was this place? There was no way this was a hotel, and if they had been found by the police or even some social agency, the surroundings still didn't make sense.

And where was Mai?

He pushed up on his elbows, careful not to hit his head again, and examined his surroundings more carefully. The walls were featureless beyond the light behind him. He searched for anything that might indicate an opening but found nothing, though the fact he was in here meant there had to be a way out. Either the top opened like a coffin, or one of the walls opened out like an overhead bin on an airplane.

He listened and all he could hear was a faint hum that matched a vibration that had gone unnoticed until now. His eyes shot wide. He was in some sort of vehicle. It could be a truck or a train, perhaps a plane. He couldn't be sure. All he knew was that this wasn't good. Something was horribly wrong. Bridgette wasn't some party girl that had drugged them just to have fun. They had been set up from the beginning and had been kidnapped.

His chest tightened, his heart pounding as images of Mai being raped by a gang of strange men overwhelmed him. "Mai, can you hear me?"

Nothing.

He took a deep breath and shouted as loud as he possibly could. "Mai! It's Tommy!"

Again, nothing.

Suddenly there was a sound to his left. He flipped over on his side to face it. The wall dropped away, light flooding in, and he squinted then gasped at the first thing he noticed.

The barrel of a gun pointed at him.

"Well, look who's awake," said a man in a thick French accent. "Our American VIP."

"Where's my girlfriend? Where's Mai?"

"Your concern is touching. You were the first thing she asked about as well."

"Is she all right?"

"As all right as you are."

He wasn't sure how to take that, but at least she was alive. "What's going on? Why have you taken us?"

"My friend, you haven't been taken. You've been purchased, and so has your girlfriend. A record sum from what I hear. Those Arabs definitely love their Americans. You're going to be in for a really good time." Tommy backed away and the man laughed. "You don't get it, do you? You and your girlfriend are now slaves, bought and paid for. Your lives are over, and I highly recommend that you not cause any trouble and cooperate with your new master. Otherwise, the living hell you're about to experience will be far worse."

Tommy recoiled in horror "You mean we're sex slaves?"

"Exactly. You catch on quick."

"You can't do this to us. I'm an American. So is my girlfriend. We've done nothing wrong! You can't do this to us!"

The man laughed. "It's the fact you're both Americans that got such a high price. Now, we don't like to damage the merchandise before we deliver it to the successful bidder, especially when the price is so high, but if you cause any trouble, I will shoot you. Now, I am the Caretaker. You can come out, use the bathroom, and get some food and water. Cause any trouble and I'll leave you in there until we reach our destination. You'll be hungry, thirsty, and covered in your own filth by the time we get there. It's your choice."

"I want to see Mai."

"Funny, she said the same thing and I'll give you the same answer I gave her. No. Nobody sees anybody. Now, are we going to do this the easy way or the hard way?"

Tommy closed his eyes and sighed, resigning himself to his fate. "The easy way."

Toussaint Residence

Paris, France

October 9, 1898

Isabelle lay curled in a ball on Caroline's bed. She had cried through much of the night before finally passing out from the drink and exhaustion. Caroline lay beside her as she had throughout the night and ran her fingers through Isabelle's hair.

"How are you doing?"

Isabelle sniffed. "Horrible. Not only did the man I love break my heart, but I have a hangover worse than I've ever had."

Caroline giggled. "Well, you did have quite a bit of champagne last night. Certainly more than you're used to. Come drink some water, it'll help."

Isabelle sat up and Caroline poured a glass of water from a pitcher sitting on the nightstand. Isabelle took a sip and swished it around her mouth then winced. "Did I throw up last night?"

Caroline groaned. "The moment you stepped out of the carriage from the party. Don't worry, you weren't the only one. You set off a bit of a chain reaction. Richard and Guy also threw up, so did Angeline."

"And *you* didn't?"

"You know me, I never throw up."

Isabelle smiled weakly. "You're like a rock."

"Well, my stomach is."

Isabelle downed the glass of water and Caroline refilled it.

"We should get you cleaned up and home. I have your overnight bag."

Isabelle's eyes narrowed. "How did you get that?"

"It was in Jacques' carriage. I had the coachman transfer it when we reached the drop-off point."

Isabelle smiled gratefully at her friend. "Thank God one of us was thinking." She sighed. "I remember it now. Oh, I made such a fool of myself! I don't think I can ever show my face again in public."

"Nonsense. You wouldn't believe how many girls were crying as they were climbing out of those carriages. You were definitely not the only person to have their heart broken last night, though I know that's little comfort. None of your friends think any less of you, I can assure you. Jacques, on the other hand, the jury's still out."

For Isabelle, it wasn't. "I don't want to ever see him again."

"That's your right, of course, though I will say one thing in his defense."

Isabelle bristled. "Is there a defense?"

"You two are just friends. You've never told him how you feel, so what he did last night wasn't a violation of some trust established between the two of you. While it is heartbreaking, of course, just remember, he didn't cheat on you. Also, we don't really know what happened. Richard's description wasn't entirely accurate. Guy said the girl dragged Jacques off the dance floor and kissed him, not the other way around. There's a very good chance he's not at fault at all and could have extricated himself from the situation soon after we left. He could be worried sick, wondering where you are."

Isabelle batted away the notion. "If that were true, then why isn't he here? He would have quickly realized all five of us had left then taken a carriage to the drop-off point. He would have seen that Richard and Guy's carriages were gone, then come here to check on me. Or he went home with that tramp."

A carriage crunched through the gravel of the courtyard outside and Caroline rushed to the window, pulling the curtain aside. "That's odd. It's Richard and Guy."

Isabelle gasped as she looked down at herself. "I have to make myself presentable!"

Caroline pointed at the overnight bag sitting on a nearby chair. "There are your things. You know where the bathroom is. Get yourself ready. I'll go see what they want." Caroline put on a housecoat, covering herself up before rushing out the door. Isabelle grabbed her bag and headed to the bathroom, quickly changing and straightening herself. She looked like death warmed over, but at least she was presentable. She repacked her bag then returned it to Caroline's bedroom before heading downstairs, finding her three friends huddled together, whispering. They fell quiet as they noticed her, and she stopped before she reached the bottom of the stairs, spotting the concern on their faces.

"What? What's wrong?"

Caroline rushed forward, a hand extended. Isabelle took it and climbed down the last few steps.

"What's going on? You're scaring me."

Caroline clasped Isabelle's hand in both of hers. "Now, there's no reason to panic yet. We don't know what's going on, but there's some news about Jacques."

Isabelle tensed, a painful lump forming in her throat. "What? What's happened?" Visions of Pierre's decapitated corpse sprung to mind. "Is he all right?"

Richard stepped forward. "I'm sure he is, however, we received a messenger this morning from his parents, asking if he was with us. Apparently, he never came home, and after waiting for hours, the coachman returned to report this fact to Mr. and Mrs. Blanchet."

Isabelle collapsed backward, her feet bumping into the bottom step, causing her to drop. Caroline, still holding her hand, guided her to a seated position as Richard and Guy rushed forward. "Something's happened to him." Bile filled her mouth. "Somebody's killed him, just like Pierre."

"Now, I'm sure that's not true," said Richard. "You're jumping to conclusions. There is an alternative that none of you want to say, but I'll say it because I'm new to the group. Jacques may have gone home with that girl he met."

Caroline glared at him. "How could you say that in front of her?"

"Hey, we're all thinking it, and isn't it better than the alternative? Wouldn't you rather he betrayed a friend's secret love for him than be lying in some alleyway without a head?"

Guy scowled at him. "That's enough. That's our friend you're talking about, so I think a little restraint is in order here." He turned to Isabelle and Caroline. "He's right about one thing. We *are* jumping to conclusions here. We need more facts. I propose we take the carriage to the pickup point and see if he's there. And if there's anyone else still hanging around, we'll ask them if they saw anything. Then we'll go to his house and talk to his parents. His father is a patron of the police, so I have no doubt every resource available will be assigned until he's found." He nodded at them. "Why don't you two get ready? If we're lucky, our foolish friend is desperately waiting for someone to pick him up."

Isabelle agreed and stood, though as she climbed the stairs, her entire being told her it was a lost cause. Jacques was dead, just like Pierre, and the plans she had secretly made with the man she had loved for so long were now torn asunder by a madman.

Paris Police Headquarters, 1 rue de Lutèce

Paris, France

Present Day

Reading held the door open for Humphrey as she flashed a smile at him. "I love working with you old guys. Chivalry still has its place."

He grunted. "Don't you forget it. I'll never be made to feel guilty over holding a door for someone just because that someone thinks every old tradition is an affront to their wokeness."

"Don't get me started on that bullshit," said Humphrey. "I just hope ten or twenty years from now when society has found something new to be offended by, all these people trying to destroy careers today get nailed for what the next generation thinks they should have been woke about."

"Let's hope."

They presented their credentials to the desk sergeant and he pointed at some chairs. "The inspector is expecting you. She'll be down in a moment."

"Thank you," said Humphrey.

They headed for the chairs and only had to wait a few minutes before a woman emerged from a side door and called their names. They rose and the woman smiled civilly. "Agents Reading and Humphrey, I'm Inspector Fontaine. I'm surprised to see two Interpol agents from London here on such a trivial matter. Is the Paris office not staffed with qualified agents?"

Humphrey cut Reading off before he could cause an international incident. "The two people involved are personal friends, so some leeway was granted."

"I understand, and I hope you understand your leeway is my waste of time. Two American tourists who attend an illegal party then don't check in with Mommy and Daddy the next day are not a concern in any country until they've been missing for at least two days. I have, however, had their photos put out to all the hospitals and shelters in the area, and the officers on the street, so everyone is keeping an eye out for them. I'm sure they'll turn up. And if they haven't by tomorrow night, then we'll open an investigation."

"Then you won't mind if we begin our own investigation in the meantime."

"I absolutely would mind, however, in the spirit of cooperation, you're free to investigate as long as you don't require any of our resources. We're stretched thin as it is."

Reading took the win. "Agreed, as long as, if we find evidence that a crime has been committed, you'll launch an official investigation."

"Of course. Assuming I agree with that evidence."

"Of course. So, I suppose that means having an officer assigned as a guide is out of the question?"

"I suggest, Agent Reading, that if you require a guide, you consult Google Maps. Now, if you'll excuse me, I have work to do." She turned on her heel and headed back through the pass-controlled door she had emerged from only minutes ago.

Humphrey patted Reading on the arm. "Congratulations."

"What?"

"That's about as calm as I've ever seen you react to a load of bollocks like that."

He grunted. "If it weren't Tommy and Mai, I might've raised a stink, but I don't want to do anything that might jeopardize their cooperation if we find anything."

Humphrey looked about. "Now what do we do?"

"We need a guide, and I think I might know how to get one."

Potomac Airfield

Fort Washington, Maryland

Laura sat in the plush leather seat and buckled her lap belt as James sat across from her, doing the same. The flight attendant walked down the aisle of the private jet, part of the lease-share network Laura had had a membership in for years. The woke crowd was now frowning upon private jet use, and it was just that type of lunacy destroying modern society. Every flight she took, her travel agent automatically bought carbon offset credits, but more importantly, where did the outrage end?

If the woke crowd managed to ban private jets, would they then turn their sights on first class, then business class? After all, those people were paying a premium that the average person couldn't afford. This false moral outrage over successful people being successful just showed how naïve these people were. If you hate the rich so much, then don't work for their companies, don't buy their products, don't work for their subsidiaries or any of their suppliers, don't benefit from any of their patents. If you hate the rich so much, put down that phone or tablet that their companies made, turn off the TV and shut down the Internet, and delete your social media accounts. Because, after all, if those people are so bad, then you shouldn't support them financially by buying their products or using their services.

It seemed today that everyone wanted to get pissed off about everything. They weren't happy unless they were angry. People had to calm down, take a breath, and examine their own lives rather than spend so much time finding something to nitpick about someone you were jealous of. The binary society that James always referred to had created a generation of hate, and she just prayed that people woke up sooner rather than later.

But right now, she had bigger problems to worry about. They still hadn't heard from Tommy and Mai, and now her concern had turned into genuine fear. Mai was so dear to her, to them both, and so was Tommy. They had sent them to a foreign country, and now something might have happened to them. If they were hurt or worse, she would never forgive herself.

James reached forward and tapped her knee. "Hon, do you want anything?"

She flinched. "What?"

He gestured toward the flight attendant, standing patiently beside their seats. "Do you want anything before we take off?"

"Oh, sorry. Mineral water with lime."

"I'll get that right out to you." The flight attendant disappeared in the galley and James leaned forward as the plane began to taxi.

"Are you all right?"

Her eyes burned with tears and her shoulders shook. "No. If anything's happened to them..." She couldn't finish the sentence.

James took her hands and gently squeezed. "I know how you feel, but right now we're both assuming the worst. For all we know, there's still an innocent explanation to this."

Laura shook her head. "It's been too long. If they had stayed somewhere else, they would have called us. If they had been mugged and their phones taken, there'd be a police report by now that Hugh would know about, or they'd be back at the hotel." She sniffed, pinching the bridge of her nose. "Something's happened to them. Something's definitely happened to them."

James patted her hand. "Then perhaps it's time to call in the big guns."

On the Open Road, Virginia

CIA Operations Officer Dylan Kane moaned in pleasure as the engine of the Harley Davidson Fat Boy sent vibrations through his entire body. He had been on motorcycles countless times in his career, but they were usually racing bikes meant to get him from point A to B as rapidly as possible, often while dodging bullets or larger ordnance. But to ride a Hog purely for pleasure was an entirely different experience.

His girlfriend, Lee Fang, was riding just behind him on a Honda CBR 250, this little road trip arranged by her as a surprise. He had been out of the country on an op for the past week and had a few days off. She always liked to surprise him with unusual experiences. Quite often they were adrenaline-fueled like car racing, skydiving, or rock climbing, but this was just pure relaxation, riding down the open road with the wind in his face and over one hundred horsepower between his legs.

This was bliss.

The only thing that could make it any better would be to recreate an Aerosmith video, though that probably wasn't wise.

His CIA-customized TAG Heuer watch sent an electrical pulse through his wrist in a pattern that indicated his private communications network had received an urgent message from a priority contact.

He cursed.

"What's wrong?" asked Fang over the radio.

"Just got an urgent message. Let's pull over." He checked his mirrors then pulled off to the side of the road and came to a stop, Fang pulling up beside him as he entered the coded sequence to unlock the message.

He groaned.

"What is it?" asked Fang.

"It's from Professor Acton."

Fang rolled her eyes. "What now? Between him and the Agency, you never get any downtime."

He pulled out his phone and logged into his secure messaging app, bringing up the message, his eyebrows rising slightly. "Well, looks like the docs are innocent in all this. Tommy and Mai have gone missing in Paris." He handed her the phone so she could read the message herself. She squinted at it.

"It hasn't even been twenty-four hours. I think they're...what did you call it? They're a bunch of worrywarts?"

He laughed. "Oh, they're definitely that, especially Laura. But it *is* out of character for those two to go incommunicado for so long. And if Reading is taking it serious enough to actually go to Paris, then there might be something behind it." He brought up the attachment showing the photo of the rave invitation. "I've heard about these raves. I've even gone to a couple in different cities. They can get pretty crazy, and some of them are fronts."

"For what?"

"Blackmail, drug dealing, human trafficking. The underground ones are never done because someone just wants to throw a party. There's always something behind them."

Fang pursed her lips. "Doesn't exactly sound like the type of thing those two would be interested in."

Kane had to agree. It was completely out of character, but that was exactly what vacations were for, to do things you wouldn't normally do. An invitation to a rave in the catacombs of Paris could prove irresistible to two young people out for an adventure. And it would never occur to them it would be dangerous. They would think they're out to have a bit of fun and then have a story to talk about for years. He had no doubt if he and Fang were in Paris and had wrangled an invitation, they would be going too, but they knew how to take care of themselves. Tommy and Mai were naïve civilians. He was CIA, and Fang was ex-Chinese Special Forces.

"What are you going to do?"

He shook his phone. "It says here the French police aren't being too cooperative. It could be as simple as getting our hands on the footage around where this rave took place. We should be able to see them arriving and leaving, then maybe we can follow them to wherever they ended up and Hugh can go over and shake them awake."

Fang sighed. "So, we're heading to Bethesda?"

"I don't see that we have much choice. There's no way the Chief would authorize the use of government resources for something as thin as this. Chris' team has the weekend off. I say, if we're ruining our road trip, we should ruin their plans as well."

Fang grinned. "Absolutely."

Firing Range, CIA Headquarters
Langley, Virginia

CIA Analyst Supervisor Chris Leroux squeezed the trigger repeatedly, firing until the mag of the Glock he gripped was spent. He could feel his hand going wildly out of control, most of the rounds beyond the first missing his target by a long shot.

His girlfriend, CIA Operations Officer Sherrie White, giggled beside him. "That was terrible! I think you actually put a couple of rounds in my target."

"Oh, and you did better the first time?"

She shrugged. "I'll never tell. The whole idea with this, remember, is not necessarily accuracy."

"Well then, I've got that part of it down pat."

She gave him a look. "*Some* is necessary. If you want accuracy, you aim, shoot, aim, shoot, because you're trying to kill somebody. But in this exercise, you're trying to get yourself out of a situation. You're taking your first shot at your target who's trying to kill you, you hope you hit him, but if you don't, you want him to keep his head down while you make your escape. If you can learn to empty a mag in the vicinity of your target, he won't be able to get an aimed shot off at you while you find cover."

"You really think I'll ever need this?"

She stared at him. "After everything you've been through, you can actually ask me that with a straight face?"

He chuckled. "Yeah, I suppose you're right. One of these days, either you or Dylan's going to get me killed."

She patted his cheek. "Not if you learn these skills. You might be the one doing the killing."

He frowned. "Not sure how I feel about that."

She reloaded his weapon. "When they're trying to kill you, any foibles you have about killing them will disappear pretty damn quickly."

"I suppose." His phone pinged with a message and he fished it from his pocket. "It's Dylan." He brought it up in his secure app, his frown deepening the further he read.

"What's wrong?"

"Looks like Tommy and Mai might be missing in Paris. They went to some rave last night and nobody's heard from them since."

Sherrie grunted. "I've been to some ragers and didn't come out for days."

"That's you. This is totally out of character for them."

"Yeah, they do seem a little straight-laced for a multi-day rager. So, what's he looking for?"

"He says he and Fang are heading for his ops center, and they're looking for volunteers to help trace them."

Sherrie shrugged. "I'd rather fire off a few hundred more rounds, but Tommy's a good kid and Mai seems nice. And he's come in when we've been up shit's creek."

Leroux fired off a reply to Kane.

On our way.

Sherrie lined up half a dozen mags, standing them upright on the counter, then held up his weapon in her left hand, her own in her right. "Now, we've got these rounds, so let's put them to use." She rapidly fired both weapons, ejecting the empty mags, then dropped both guns down, the upright mags slipping into place, and she was firing again less than a second later. She repeated the process until all the ammo was spent and everyone at the range had stopped what they were doing to watch the display put on by the unassuming hottie. She blew at the tips of both barrels as if in an old Western. "Now, that was fun." She cleared her weapons as Leroux basked in her awesomeness, still amazed that this incredible woman loved him. She returned the weapons to their case then faced him. "*Now* we go find our friends. Your training is done for the day, Padawan."

He grinned.

So hot, and she could make accurate Star Wars references.

Paris Police Headquarters, 1 rue de Lutèce

Paris, France

A black Peugeot SUV shuddered to a halt in front of them and Reading instinctively put an arm out to protect his partner. The passenger window rolled down and a young man with several days' growth of facial hair and a scruffy coiffure leaned over.

"Are you Hugh and Michelle?"

Reading nodded. "We're Agents Reading and Humphrey."

The man batted a hand. "Titles and surnames are for strangers, and we're going to be friends." He grinned. "I'm Sasha. I'm your guide. Mary sent me." He jerked a thumb toward the back seat. "Hop in."

Humphrey rolled her eyes at Reading but climbed in. Reading followed and they were peeling away from the curb before he could get the door shut.

"The briefing I got was brief. Apparently, you have two friends missing since last night, and our friendly police aren't being too cooperative."

94

Reading grunted. "You could say that."

Humphrey's response was more useful. "They won't open an investigation until it's been forty-eight hours or there's evidence something untoward has happened."

"So, we're looking for evidence?"

"Yes."

"And where would you like to start looking?"

Reading read off the address from the photo of the invitation, and Sasha's eyes narrowed in the rearview mirror. "Odd place. Are you sure that's where you want to go?"

"Apparently, there was a rave in the catacombs last night that our friends may have attended."

"Ah, yes, those are very illegal. The police are always trying to find them, but they rarely do, and they almost never find the organizers. I have a friend who went to one a few months ago. He said the setup was like a club, laser show, smoke machines, strobe lights, professional sound system, DJ. You have to wonder what's in it for them."

"What do you mean?" asked Humphrey.

"I mean, it's not cheap to set all that up, and they don't charge a cover fee. And sometimes there's alcohol and drugs just being given away. So, if they're not making money at the event, how are they paying for it?"

Humphrey shrugged. "The Great Gatsby?"

Sasha smiled. "Ah, yes. Great movie. Apparently, there's a book too." Reading was about to insult a generation when Sasha laughed. "Ha! Got you! The book was better. Now, a rich guy throwing parties, that's definitely a possibility, but my job is to keep an ear close to the ground. Word is starting to spread to not go to these parties."

This caught Reading's attention. "Why not?"

"I don't know. I've just heard from two different sources that deal with street kids that word is spreading to not attend these events."

"Interesting. Whatever the reason is, it would have to be pretty serious for street kids to give up a free party."

Sasha agreed. "Maybe the reason is the same one behind why your friends are missing."

"Do you think we could talk to some of these kids?"

Sasha shrugged. "I can take you to some of the places they hang out and you can talk *at* them, but there's no guarantee they'll talk *with* you. They don't like police."

"Then we won't tell them we're police. We'll just say we're a husband and wife looking for our daughter and her boyfriend."

Sasha gave Reading a long stare in the rearview mirror then laughed. "Do you really think you could pull off husband and wife? Father and daughter, maybe."

Humphrey grinned at Reading. "Maybe I've got daddy issues."

Reading growled at them both. "Fine. Father and daughter. We're looking for her sister and boyfriend. Satisfied?"

Humphrey patted him on the knee. "Yes, Daddy."

Blanchet Residence

Paris, France

October 9, 1898

Leblanc flipped through his notes, frowning. When the richest of the rich had a concern, demands were made, and the entire police force was expected to drop everything for what was quite often a trivial matter. But today was something different. Another young man of Paris' elite was missing, the fourth in the past two months, and this time it had just happened and his friends were cooperating fully.

Earlier this morning, they had conducted several interviews with Pierre Joliette's family and friends, which had proved fruitless. He was estranged from his family and his brother was a known troublemaker who refused to cooperate. What few friends they were able to find knew nothing, but this group that sat in front of him now were also friends of Pierre, and his latest possible victim, a victim who had apparently secured an invitation to some secret party.

"And you have no idea where the party was?" asked a skeptical Archambault.

Guy shook his head. "No, that's the whole point of it. The invitation gives you an address that you go to, and there are carriages there waiting to take you to the party."

"And is the party in the same place every time?"

"From the descriptions I've heard, including from Pierre, yes, it's always the same place. The pickup place changes every time, though."

"So, this is a bi-weekly thing?"

"As far as I know. This is the only time we've ever managed to get an invitation."

"And how long has this been going on?"

Guy shrugged. "I first heard of it a few weeks ago. I don't think very long or at least one of us would have heard about it. It's hard to keep something like this a secret."

Isabelle, apparently, finally had enough, the one person in the group who appeared to be taking it harder than all the others. "Is he dead?"

Everyone stopped talking and Leblanc regarded her. "We have no evidence either way. However, his disappearance does follow a pattern. Three others have been reported missing then found dead, including your friend, Pierre, all part of Paris' elite, all young males around Jacques' age, and at least three of the four having attended a mysterious party before their disappearance. That can't be a coincidence, and unfortunately, if it isn't, then it likely means your friend has fallen victim as well. That, however, doesn't mean he's necessarily dead yet. We need to find this château, because whoever is throwing these parties, I believe, is our killer."

Richard folded his arms. "And just how do you propose to find this place?"

Leblanc nodded at his partner, not much older than the others in the room. "I think you need to secure my friend here an invitation."

Kane's Off-the-Books Operations Center

Outside Bethesda, Maryland

Present Day

There was no hiding their arrival on his Hog and her crotch rocket. They did a circuit of the storage area, finding no one in plain sight, then parked their bikes in a secluded area where they couldn't be seen from the road. They walked to the two storage containers he had customized. From the outside, they were nothing special, but inside was a state-of-the-art operations center he had set up just in case shit fell apart. Over recent years, it had been used far more often than he had ever thought it would be.

Fang covered him as he entered his code in the hidden panel. The door hissed open, the inside kept at a slightly higher air pressure to protect against chemical or biological attack. He pushed the door open and stepped inside, Fang following. She secured things behind him as he headed deeper into the complex. He began flicking switches, activating all the equipment, and they were online within minutes.

He turned to Fang. "Double-check our supplies. Make sure we've got enough for five days."

"I thought you had enough for months?"

"I do, but anything could have happened. Chris and Sherrie could have turned this into a love nest."

Fang snickered. "Now that I'd pay to see."

Kane eyed her. "So, you like to watch, huh?"

She gave him a look. "You know what I mean."

"Oh, you like to watch. I'm going to have to put that to use somehow."

"You're terrible. I'm going to check on the supplies." She motioned at one of the security feeds. "It looks like Sonya's here."

Sonya Tong, a senior analyst at the CIA and second-in-command of Leroux's team at Langley, was one of the few people who actually knew the location of the off-the-books operations center. They trusted her implicitly. Kane waited for her to reach the door then he buzzed her in, saving her having to enter the code. Tong smiled up at the camera then stepped inside. The door clicked shut.

"Hello?"

"I'm in ops," called Kane.

"I'm just checking supplies," said Fang. "Just in case someone ate everything between the last time we were here and now."

Kane watched on one of the internal security cameras as Tong walked down the corridor then tossed her go-bag in one of the sleeping quarters before joining him.

"Hey, Dylan. Keeping out of trouble?"

He grinned. "I keep trying, but the Chief keeps throwing me back into the ring."

She plunked down in one of the chairs in front of the workstations. "So, what do we know?"

"Not very much, and this could all be a wild goose chase, but every hour that passes has me leaning toward Laura's belief that something's gone wrong. You know Tommy, he's obsessed with social media, and he and Mai aren't exactly crazy partiers."

Tong shrugged. "You'd be surprised what you do when you're on vacation that you wouldn't do if you thought somebody you knew would see you."

Kane eyed her. "Sonya! Are you a secret party girl?"

"If I told you I'd have to kill you."

He roared with laughter as Fang entered the room. "I'm learning all kinds of things today. Sonya's a secret party girl, and Fang likes to watch."

They both gave him the finger.

He raised his hands in mock surrender. "Fine, fine. Let's get serious here. Here's what we know so far. Tommy posted a picture of a paper invitation to what we assume was an illegal rave held in the catacombs of Paris. He posted this around ten-thirty PM local last night. They were then seen leaving the hotel at around eleven, and that's the last time they were seen. Their phones have been offline since around midnight with no social media posts since and no other forms of contact. The driver sent to the hotel to take them to a prearranged location this morning reported that he couldn't make contact with them, and the professors' travel agent, Mary, had the hotel check on them and they found the room empty and not slept in. Jim and Laura are on a plane heading for Paris, Agent Reading and his partner Michelle Humphrey are already there, and the French police aren't being cooperative, though I don't really blame them. As far as they're concerned, there's no case here yet."

"So, what's our job?" asked Tong.

"Make a case. I want us to hack every camera we can find. There has to be footage of them going to that rave and coming out of it." He tapped the image of the invitation displayed on one of the monitors. "I want to backtrack their movements as well. Somebody gave them that invitation. Find out who that person was and we might have a lead."

Tong turned toward her workstation. "You know who I wish was here to help us with this?"

Kane glanced at her. "Tommy?"

"Yes, Tommy. He's better at this than anybody I know."

"Well, from what Chris tells me, you're the best at what you do, so let's get this show on the road."

Rave Invitation Location

Paris, France

Reading looked about at what wasn't a great part of town, and was certainly somewhere he couldn't see Tommy and Mai going, either willingly or wittingly.

"They had to have taken a cab here," said Humphrey.

Reading shook his head. "No, apparently they headed for the Métro when they left the hotel last night."

Sasha's eyes narrowed. "Really? I thought they were staying at the Ritz."

"They are."

"Well, to get from there to here is not exactly a simple thing. You're talking several transfers, and I didn't see any instructions on that invitation. Somebody had to tell them how to get here."

"Or they looked it up."

"True. I guess Google could have gotten them here." Sasha gestured at several businesses. "Some of these should have cameras, and the Métro definitely does."

Reading agreed and sent his GPS location to Kane with a few photos of the area.

Check for cameras.

A thumbs-up came back a moment later.

"So, how would you access the catacombs from here?" asked Humphrey.

Sasha stood, surveying the area with his hands on his hips. "It wouldn't be on the street. It's too exposed and would draw too much attention."

"Would it be through one of these businesses? Their basements?"

"No, absolutely not. None of them would willingly let that many undesirables through their business in the middle of the night to take part in an illegal party. And if it had been done without them knowing, they would have found out this morning and filed a police report that even your uncooperative inspector would have been made aware of if she did even the briefest of checks on your story. No, they'd be accessing it through the city sewers or drainage system." He pointed at a nearby manhole cover. "Through one of these, but out of sight in one of the alleyways."

"How will we know which one?" asked Reading, at least half a dozen alleyways within sight.

"It might not be possible to tell, depending on how well they cleaned up after themselves." Sasha paused for a moment. "Wait right here." He darted across the street toward a cafe with a small patio, just three tables, one occupied by half a dozen young people, all of them likely to fit right in at an underground rave. Words were exchanged and a fifty euro note appeared, followed by more words before someone pointed toward an alleyway and the money was handed over.

Sasha rejoined them. "They said the party was down that alleyway, through the manhole cover, down the ladder, hang a right, go through a door and you're in the catacombs." He glanced at their shoes. "I don't think you're exactly dressed for it."

"I'll expense a new pair of shoes if I have to," said Reading.

Sasha grinned. "Good, we're on an expense account. Put me down for fifty euros."

Unknown Location

"Can I have something to wear?" Mai's voice trembled as she struggled to cover her private parts with her hands and arms.

Her captor leered at her. "Sweetheart, the better part of the rest of your life will be spent naked. I highly recommend you get used to it. Besides, you've got a gorgeous body, you've got nothing to be ashamed about."

She glared at him. "Just because someone has a good body doesn't give you the right to stare at it."

He smirked. "Spirit. That's good. They like that. They especially like to beat it out of you. If you want to live, you have to keep them interested. The longer they find you interesting, the longer they want to play with you."

"Play?" Her skin crawled.

"You're now someone's toy. What they do with you is up to them. It might be sexual, it might be something different. Whatever it is, I can guarantee you won't like it. All you have to do is keep them interested

107

and you'll live. Try to escape or cross them in some way, and you'll find yourself either dead or sold to someone else. The further down the line that you're sold, the more broken you become, and the less interested they are in enjoying you for what you are. Eventually, you'll just be a piece of meat that someone will decide to carve up just to hear you scream. So, me staring at you while you walk around here naked is the least of your worries." He pointed at the bathroom at the far end of what she was certain was a semitrailer. "Now, use the bathroom, drink your water, get something to eat, then get back in bed. You've got ten minutes."

Mai decided to pick her battles with the man who had called himself the Caretaker. She desperately had to go to the bathroom. This had been the first opportunity since she had been kidnapped, and she didn't know when the next might come. She did her business then took the opportunity to wash up. She still felt grimy from last night's sweaty dance floor experience in the catacombs, brief flashes continuing to remind her of what had happened.

And it all disgusted her.

She dried her hands then the vehicle they were in braked suddenly and her hand darted out, pressing against the wall to steady herself. There was a surge as they regained speed, as if it had been cut off in traffic.

She had to now think critically rather than emotionally if she were to survive this. She had no intention of becoming a sex slave. She'd kill herself before she'd let that happen, but she wasn't there yet. She was still being transported, and because it was by truck, it would take time, time for her to figure a way out of this, time for her to find Tommy, time for the professors and their friends to intervene. She just had to survive and be smart. She had to remain fully aware of her surroundings, for when the opportunity did come, she'd have to be ready to take advantage.

She emerged from the bathroom and decided to forego the pointless attempt to cover herself. She had to get used to it. Not because she intended to be enslaved for the rest of her life, but because when she did make her escape attempt, she couldn't be concerned with who might see her naked body.

Her captor ogled her as she ate several prepackaged food items, downing them with a bottle of orange juice. "I'm happy to see you've accepted your situation."

She shrugged as she continued to eat. "There's no point in being hungry." She grabbed several power bars, a couple of bottles of water, and a Gatorade. "Can I bring these back to bed with me?"

"Yes, just don't drink too much. Your next bathroom break isn't for four hours."

"What if I need to go before?"

"Pee in a bottle."

She gave him a look and put her hands on her hips, thrusting them to one side. "You mean to tell me that if I knock on the door, you won't open it so you can get another look at this?"

He leered at her, taking in every square inch of her body except her face, as if she were the piece of meat he had referred to earlier. "Fine. If you need to come out, just knock."

"Thank you."

He pulled out his phone and took several photos of her. "Turn around."

She turned, squeezing her eyes shut, holding back the tears as this pig created masturbatory material.

"All right, get back in your pod."

She climbed back into her prison cell, one of twelve she had counted. Her captor reached out to close the panel to seal her in when she turned back to face him, giving him a full view of her body. "Tell me one thing."

"What's that?"

"Is my boyfriend here?"

"And what do I get if I tell you?"

She glanced down at her breasts. "One touch."

His nostrils flared then he pointed up. "He's right on top of you, sweetheart." He leaned in and placed his mouth on her breast and she gasped in shock as it wasn't the type of touch she had meant. Her mouth filled with bile as he worked her nipple and she smacked him on the top of his head. "That's enough!"

He pulled away and she forced a smile, the look he gave her terrifying. "You and I might just have a lot of fun on this trip."

"How long a trip is it?"

"Long enough."

"Where are we going?"

He wagged a finger. "That kind of information takes a lot more than a touch, but I will say this. I hope you have your sea legs." He cackled as he pulled down the lid, sealing her back inside her prison. She immediately poured some of the water from one of the bottles onto her hand then cleaned off her breast, wiping it dry with the comforter. She steadied her stomach then lay back, her entire body racked with sobs, for what had just happened to her was nothing compared to the life she had in store for her. She pressed her hand against the top of her prison, her eyes squeezed shut.

"Tommy."

The Catacombs

Paris, France

Reading stood in the center of where the party must have taken place, though if it had, he still hadn't spotted any evidence of it, the cleanup job remarkably well done. Sasha was the first to notice a clue something had happened here.

He pointed. "There we go, that's what I've been looking for."

Reading and Humphrey joined him, Humphrey shining the flashlight from her phone at where Sasha was pointing, revealing two tiny holes that clearly didn't belong.

"What am I looking at?" asked Reading.

"There was a clip here to hold a cable." Sasha ran his finger along the wall then pointed at another one. "You're going to find these all over the place. They had this place wired. A sound system, for sure. Probably a light show, maybe even cameras. Who knows? But the fact they wired this then took everything down, not even leaving the clips, means this was well organized."

Reading scratched his chin. "You would think people hosting an illegal party wouldn't be too concerned about cleaning up after themselves. They would just grab their equipment and leave." He waved a hand at the chamber. "There's not a bottle, a cup, nothing. They clearly didn't want anybody to know they were here."

Humphrey agreed. "It makes sense, if you think about it. If they were doing these raves and leaving the catacombs damaged, or a mess that had to be cleaned up with taxpayer money, then the police might get more involved. But if all you have is an illegal party and the next day no evidence it had ever happened, then the police have more important things to do than track down some scofflaws."

Reading frowned. "Let's get out of here. The only way we're finding anything is if we send in a forensics team, and there's no way our French friends are going to do that until we get some evidence of a real crime."

They made their way out of the catacombs and back into the city system then up the ladder to the surface. Reading leaned against a wall, struggling to regain his breath. He was still recovering from what had happened to him in Thailand and the damage done to his heart from a blockage he had had for years, now opened by a stent. His stamina was far better than it had been in years, but his workouts hadn't included ladders and balancing acts along thin ledges.

"Are you all right?" asked Humphrey, concern in her voice.

"I will be, but next time you go in and take pictures for me."

She laughed. "Sounds good. Let's get you back to the car."

They walked back to the SUV, Reading shaking off any help. He climbed in the passenger seat and Sasha fired up the engine and the air conditioning.

"I'll be back in a moment." Sasha stepped out of the car, darting into a shop across the street.

"Are you feeling any better?" asked Humphrey from the back seat.

Reading nodded. "Yeah, I'm still catching my breath a bit, but I'll be fine. Outside of my rehab, that's the most physical activity I've had since Thailand."

"And that nearly killed you."

He grunted. "You have no idea." He hadn't given her all the details of what had happened there, though he had given her enough to know it had been a hellish experience in too many ways. But he wasn't going to let his physical condition deter him from saving Mai and Tommy, even if it killed him.

Some things were worth dying for.

The driver-side door opened, startling him, and Sasha dropped into his seat, closing the door. He held up a couple of cloth bags. "I have water, juice, energy drinks. I have crisps, as you Brits call them, power bars, chocolate bars, and a few sandwiches. Let's all fuel up and discuss what we're doing next."

Reading peered into the bags and grabbed a bottle of water and a sandwich, thanking their guide. "I didn't realize how hungry I was until you mentioned the word sandwich."

Humphrey grabbed a Gatorade and a sandwich for herself, then settled into the back seat as Sasha made his own selection. "So, where do

114

we go now?" she asked as she cracked the bottle cap. "That was pretty much our only clue."

Reading agreed as he chewed his first bite, his eyebrows shooting up at the burst of flavor, this creation definitely not from a vending machine. Pride was put into it, which likely meant it was freshly made at the shop Sasha had gone into. Reading fished out his phone. "Let's see if the others have found anything."

Sasha gave him a look. "Others?"

Humphrey leaned between the seats. "It's best you don't ask too many questions."

Sasha shrugged, biting into his own sandwich. "It wouldn't be the first time I've been told to mind my own business."

Kane's Off-the-Books Operations Center

Outside Bethesda, Maryland

All four workstations in Kane's off-the-books operations center were now occupied. Leroux had taken over control of the op from Kane as soon as he had been brought up to speed, and the operative was now getting some rack time as he was the only one fresh off an op and yawning incessantly.

"We have to anticipate we'll be here for days and that we're going to need to constantly monitor," Leroux had said. "We'll come up with a rotating schedule, but I want yawny out of here before it becomes contagious."

Kane had shrugged. "Don't have to ask me twice." He grinned at Fang. "Care to join me?"

Leroux put an end to that. "Sleep, not sex. Besides, I need her. The next few hours are critical."

"I know, I know. Wake me if you need me."

So far, they hadn't. This was an exercise in hacking cameras and reviewing the feeds. Kane had an impressively large database of unsecured and cracked cameras, most people not realizing that when they installed a security camera and connected it to their Wi-Fi, if they didn't change the factory default password, anybody in the world could access it. Hackers and government agencies devoted massive amounts of hardware to crawl the Internet in search of unsecured devices, and even when they were secure, quite often, "password" or "123456" was all that prevented them from getting in. It meant a treasure trove of information was at their fingertips, and they were already reviewing footage from last night in the neighborhood where the rave had taken place.

Tong pointed at her screen. "I've got them."

Everyone stopped what they were doing and turned to watch.

"That's a subway station. They just came out of it, 23:55 local, just in time for their party. Now, let's see if they meet up with anybody."

They watched as Mai and Tommy walked hand-in-hand, smiles on their faces. It was clear they were there willingly and eagerly.

Leroux cursed as they went off screen. "Okay, we need another shot."

"I've got one. Don't worry." Tong tapped a few keys and a shot from farther down the street showed the two of them walking toward the camera. A girl emerged from a small crowd and joined them. Hugs were exchanged, a piece of paper handed over that Leroux assumed was the invitation, then she led them toward the alley where Reading had indicated the rave was taking place.

Leroux wagged a finger at the screen. "Clearly that woman knew them, and she's probably the one who invited them. She's the key to this entire thing. We have to find her. Can we get enough for facial recognition?"

Tong shook her head. "They're too far away and it's a shit camera. We need to find a better angle." She zoomed in on the image, the result a mess of pixelization, the resolution too low, the distance too far.

Leroux turned to her. "You keep reviewing those two camera angles. I want to see if any of those three come back out later. Fang, you review going backward. See if you can find any footage of that woman arriving. If she happened to come in on the same subway, we just might get a good shot of her face. Sherrie, you and I are going to try to find other cameras around the area and see if we get lucky, but first I'm going to update Reading." He wagged his phone. "He's already messaged me three times in the past five minutes, and he's definitely not the patient type."

Medici Fountain

Paris, France

Sasha approached a group of young people he claimed lived on the streets, hanging out around a fountain. Some of them looked perfectly normal to Reading, or as normal as young people looked to his generation. Scruffy clothes, messy hair, unkempt beards. They certainly didn't appear employable. He had learned over his years in policing that most of these people had a tragic story. The short-timers were sometimes runaways who got in an argument with their parents over something stupid like a boy and would soon be home, but others were escaping abuse—physical, mental, sexual. They lived on the streets because they felt it was safer than the alternative back home. He had heard them called many things, but ghosts seemed appropriate. Society could see them but looked through them. He was guilty of it despite knowing better. Most of these kids weren't the addicts that people thought they were.

They were victims.

Sasha beckoned them over and he and Humphrey joined him amid the cluster of children, most in their mid to late teens. "This is Hugh and Michelle. They're looking for two friends that disappeared last night. We know they went to that rave," said Sasha in English. He gestured at Reading. "Show them the photos."

Reading already had his tablet out and brought up a split-screen he had prepared with photos of Tommy and Mai. The teens gathered around and someone took the tablet, Reading getting the sense he might never see it again.

A girl pointed at the screen. "I remember her, she was there."

"And her boyfriend?" asked Humphrey.

"I'm not sure. I saw him from behind, but I saw her. She was definitely on something and having a good time."

Reading tensed and forced himself to remain calm. Being defensive wouldn't be helpful. "What do you think she was on?"

The girl shrugged. "Who knows? Everyone there was on something. They're just passing out laced drinks until you can't stand. It was an awesome party."

"Did you see who they were with?"

"Yeah, they were with Bridgette."

Reading suppressed his excitement. "Who's Bridgette?"

A boy Sasha had been talking to replied. "She used to be one of us and then she met somebody that organizes the parties. The only time we see her now is when she's handing out the invitations to let us know where the next one is. Sometimes she pays us bonuses if we bring in new people."

The girl swatted him. "We're not supposed to talk about that."

The boy shrugged. "What's the big deal? Are you going to tell her?"

Reading ended the squabble before it cut off the flow of information. "Does she have a last name?"

"I'm sure she does, but I don't know it."

"Any idea where we can find her?"

The girl eyed them. "Why? What are you going to do to her, arrest her?"

Humphrey chuckled. "We're not French police. We have no authority to arrest her. All we want to do is find our friends and she might be the last one who saw them before they disappeared."

The boy grunted. "They wouldn't be the first to disappear after one of those parties."

Reading's eyes narrowed. "What do you mean?"

The boy shrugged. "People are always disappearing after."

The girl swatted his shoulder again. "That's nonsense and you know it. They just went home after getting tired of being on the street. You thought Philippe had disappeared after one of the parties but he showed up two weeks later saying he had gone home and then his father beat him again so he left."

The boy shrugged. "Well, maybe then I don't know what I'm talking about. I'm just saying, I think people are disappearing. That's why I never drink anything at those parties. When you wake up the next day in some alleyway and don't remember how you got there, you know it's not a good scene."

Reading steered the conversation back to the more pertinent point. "Any idea where we can find this Bridgette? We just want to talk to her. We just want to find out what happened to our friends."

The girl shrugged. "She's around. Not much with us anymore. In a few days, she'll probably pass out a new set of invitations. I know she likes to ride the Métro. That's where she would hide out from her parents until she finally ran away. I think she feels safe there, and now that she's eighteen, nobody can touch her as long as she pays the fare."

Reading pulled out a sheaf of business cards. "There's a reward. Ten thousand euros to whoever finds me Bridgette."

Cards were snatched eagerly, and after Humphrey got a detailed description of what Bridgette looked like, they returned to the car.

Humphrey stared at him. "Ten-thousand-euro reward? I hope that's coming out of your pocket because there's no way in hell Interpol will authorize that."

"No, but Jim and Laura will, and that's just a drop in the ocean to them."

Humphrey grunted. "And you wonder why people think the justice system treats the rich differently than the poor."

Reading sighed as he took a drink of water. "Unfortunately, that's the way the world works. And right now, I'm going to use every advantage their money gives us to find those kids."

En Route to Police Headquarters

Paris, France

October 9, 1898

"Doesn't this seem a little odd?"

Leblanc regarded his partner. "What? That someone is decapitating young men? Of course I find it odd."

Archambault shook his head. "That's not what I mean. I mean, why the parties? There have to be easier ways, and certainly less expensive ways, to attract your victims. Get a man drunk in a bar, invite him for a carriage ride home, inject him, kill him. You're out a few francs. But instead, our suspect is throwing lavish parties, all just to attract a single victim each week. It doesn't make sense."

"It doesn't make sense to us, but I'm willing to bet it makes perfect sense to him. There's always method to the madness. The parties serve a purpose, and that's to attract the sons and daughters of the elite of Paris. But I'm sure there's a second purpose, some hidden meaning. Perhaps something happened to him at a party like this, something that hurt him, something that embarrassed him, and this is his revenge. We'll have to go through the old case reports and see if there were any incidents at a party at a château going back the past ten years."

"Ten years?"

"If something traumatic happened to affect someone so deeply that they turned to decapitation, it suggests a trauma from someone's youth that they weren't able to process mentally, and now they're lashing out at the world to get their revenge on it."

Archambault frowned. "I shudder to think what could have happened in someone's childhood that would twist them so much."

"As do I."

Archambault stared out the window for a moment. "You know, I was thinking about what our witnesses were saying about this pickup point."

"What about it?"

"Well, it sounded to me from the description of the party that there were hundreds of people there. How many carriage rides would that be? And didn't they say it was about a twenty-minute ride? That would be a minimum forty-minute round trip. Add loading and off-loading, and you're looking at almost an hour. You're not bringing people to a party six at a time when there are a couple of hundred there. Sounds to me like it was at least forty or fifty carriage rides. You could spread it out over a few hours, perhaps, though I would say two at most. That would mean there would have to be a couple of dozen carriages involved, wouldn't there?"

Leblanc's head slowly bobbed as he did the math, then a smile broke out. "We just might make a detective of you yet."

124

Archambault was right. There would have to be a lot of carriages involved, and each would have two horses. Few households, if any within twenty minutes of that pickup location would have stables that large, no matter how wealthy. But there was another important factor. Each one of those carriages required a coachman, and while carriages and horses could be trusted to keep quiet about what they were involved in, a dozen or two wagging tongues meant word would get around, and every one of them knew exactly where this château was.

He regarded his partner. "Let's get messages out to every single carriage for hire. I think you might have just cracked this case."

En route to France
Over the Atlantic Ocean
Present Day

Acton felt helpless. They were trapped in this airplane still several hours away from landing in Paris, and all they knew now was that Tommy and Mai had indeed been at the rave and at least Mai had been on drugs. It was totally out of character for her and he couldn't believe she would be so irresponsible or that Tommy would let her.

"She must not have known," said Laura. "I can't see her willingly taking drugs."

"Neither can I. The fact we haven't heard from either of them though, has to mean they both were drugged either willingly or unwillingly, and they could still just be sleeping it off."

Laura eyed him skeptically. "I don't know. It would be one hell of a long time to sleep one off."

Acton shrugged. "I remember sleeping through a few weekends during my college days. You wake up, you drink some water, you go back to sleep. And if you've got food handy, look out, you might not be seen for a week. What has me concerned is that even after my worst bender, I was still coherent enough by this time to have made any calls I was supposed to have made. I'm concerned about what Hugh mentioned, that one boy claiming people were disappearing from the raves."

"So am I, though the girl's explanation is as good as any. We need some piece of evidence that shows that this was something other than an innocent bout of youthful exuberance going a little too far. All we know right now is that they did go to the party, they were seen at the party, at least Mai appeared to be on drugs, and that's it."

"Don't forget this Bridgette character." Acton's eyebrows shot up with a thought. "Wait a minute. Dylan said they had footage of a girl greeting Tommy and Mai. It had to be this Bridgette person. The invitation has an address, but according to Hugh, the actual entrance to the party was through a manhole cover in a nearby alleyway. That's not indicated on the invitation and there's no way they could know where to go, so they had to be meeting her there. What do you think the chances are that there was some communication between them before they met?"

Laura pulled out her phone. "Pretty bloody good, I would think." She put the call on speaker as Leroux answered. "Chris, it's James and Laura. Have you been able to pull any records for their phones or for the hotel?"

"Unfortunately, no. If we were doing this from Langley, we'd be able to use their back doors, but unfortunately, we can't get in. The sad thing is, if there was someone who could, it would be Tommy. I do have a resource that I'm debating inviting in, but I'm not sure I trust him."

"What do you mean you don't trust him?" asked Acton.

127

"He's a kid who's got no brain-mouth filter," said Tong.

Leroux muttered something in the background. "His name's Randy Child. He's on my team. He's completely trustworthy from the standpoint of the job, it's just that he gets too excited sometimes, and he's liable to blurt out the existence of this facility."

"Would he be able to hack the phone systems?" asked Laura.

"Absolutely."

"Then don't you think it's worth the risk?"

Leroux sighed. "If it weren't Tommy and Mai, I'd say no, it's not, but you're right. We have to do whatever it takes." His voice was slowing as if he were losing his train of thought. "Just a second. I'll call you back."

The call ended and Acton sat back. "What do you think that was all about?"

Laura shook her head. "I don't know, but I got the distinct impression he just figured something out."

"Let's hope it's a way to find this Bridgette girl because I think she's the key to everything, and the longer this goes on, the less likely it is that we're going to find the kids. They could be halfway around the world by now."

Laura shivered and hugged herself, rubbing her hands on her arms. "If they were kidnapped for ransom, we would've heard something by now. The fact we haven't heard anything has to mean they were either killed or are going to be killed, or they're being trafficked." Tears flowed down her cheeks. "If something happens to them…" Her voice faded as she bit on a knuckle.

Acton leaned forward and took her other hand. "We're not going to let that happen. I don't care how much it costs or how many IOUs we need to collect on, we're going to get them back if it's the last thing we ever do."

Kane's Off-the-Books Operations Center

Outside Bethesda, Maryland

Leroux ended the call then leaned back. "Sonya, bring up the image of that invitation." Tong brought it up. "Put it on the big screens." She did and they all faced the opposite wall.

"What are you thinking?" asked Sherrie as he scanned every square inch of the enlarged image.

"Reading's message said that this Bridgette was getting bonuses for bringing in desirables to the party. If this is some kind of human trafficking thing, then two young American tourists would definitely be prime candidates. They're both young, healthy, attractive, so you'd think she'd get a bonus for bringing them in."

"Sure, Mai's gorgeous," said Fang.

Sherrie agreed. "And I'd let Tommy do me."

Leroux gave her a look and she patted him on the shoulder.

"Don't worry, dear. Only if I were single."

"Uh-huh. Anyway, like I was saying, they'd be worth a bonus, I would think. But how would they keep track of that?"

"What do you mean?"

"Well, I doubt there was a registration table taking names then asking them if they'd care to participate in a survey where they were asked how they found out about the party."

"You mean the invitation is the key."

"Exactly. I'm willing to bet there's some way to identify who gave out these invitations, either a different wording or something in the design. But even that doesn't identify prime targets." He pointed, finally spotting what he had been searching for. "There it is, top righthand corner. Do you see that?"

Sherrie rose from her chair and stepped closer, staring at the image. "What am I looking for?"

"See that red line? It looks kind of faded and out of place."

Sherrie shrugged. "There's lots of red on this. It's a flyer advertising a party. It's colorful."

Leroux laughed then rose, pointing at what he had spotted. "Doesn't that look like something's bled through the paper, like a marker from the back?"

Sherrie's jaw dropped slightly. "Huh. I can't believe I missed that."

"We all missed it, but I'm willing to bet she wrote her phone number on the back so that they could contact her, and so she'd have proof that one of her prime targets had arrived and handed in their invitation. Sonya, see if you can work your magic and analyze that photo. Maybe we can read what's on the other side."

"On it." Tong turned back toward her workstation then they all watched as the colors and text disappeared, leaving nothing but a white, slightly wrinkled paper. She then applied multiple filters, and as she continued to manipulate the image, the faint discoloration from the other side, invisible to the naked eye but not to the camera lens that had taken the photo, was slowly revealed.

Leroux folded his arms and smiled at what was clearly a phone number with the name Bridgette written above it, a small heart above the "i." "Now, we finally have a real lead."

Tong frowned. "Too bad there's not much we can do with it."

Leroux chose not to be so pessimistic. "Send that to Reading and the professors. Fang, go wake up Dylan. We need his permission to bring in Randy. I think we need a wunderkind on the team."

Fang left the room to wake Kane and Leroux gestured at Tong's workstation. "Try pinging that number. Let's see what happens."

Tong tapped at her keyboard and frowned as the response came back negative. "The phone's not on."

Leroux cursed. "And I don't think it's going to be on again. Most likely it was a burner and has already been tossed. She's already on a new phone for the next party."

Sherrie returned to her seat. "Well, that would certainly suggest she's in on it and isn't just some patsy."

"Agreed. We're definitely going to need Randy to hack the phone companies. We need to trace that phone."

"Isn't that kind of pointless now?" asked Sherrie. "I mean, if it was a burner and it's already been tossed."

"The burner's been tossed, but not her habits. They said she likes to ride the subway. I'm willing to bet she likes to ride the same routes. If we can trace that phone and see where it's been over the past week, we might be able to figure out where she likes to frequent and at least Hugh and Michelle will have a chance of finding her."

Kane stumbled into the room. "What's up?"

"We need to bring Randy in," said Leroux.

Kane frowned but acquiesced. "Fine, but if he spills the location of this facility, I'm sending you the moving bill."

The Métro

Paris, France

Bridgette yawned as she leaned against the window on the Métro, the vibrations relaxing as the train ran over the tracks. Last night had been a lot of fun and it was unfortunate it had to end the way it did. A threesome with the American tourists would have been a blast, but that hadn't been her job. It did have her horny as hell, however, and she had debated going home with Victor for a romp, but it wasn't wise to mix business with pleasure.

They were all temporary. She was useful to them while she could still bring in the desirable targets, but the moment she couldn't, they would cut her loose. She had seen it happen before. The question was, what did it mean to be cut loose? Were you allowed to leave freely to enjoy the money you had made, or were you killed then dumped in a barrel of acid with no trace of you left behind?

Or were you put up for auction?

In the debrief after, she had been told the Americans had sold as a bundle for 10 million and her 0.1% cut would be the biggest single night haul she had ever had. She was sure she was good now for at least another few months, but she was planning her exit. She had to. When she had been recruited, life had been horrible. If she had died, it would have been a blessing. But now that she was no longer living on the streets, no longer starving, no longer filthy, she wanted to live.

With this next payout, she would have enough money in her Swiss bank account to take care of herself for the rest of her life, albeit a simple middle-class existence, which was all she wanted. She had met someone a few months ago who knew how to get his hands on fake IDs. She now had all the paperwork, including a passport, and the travel plans to get herself out of Paris then out of France and into Canada, where she'd blend into the bilingual population of Montreal and live out her life, atoning for the sins she had committed to earn it.

She wasn't a bad person, at least she didn't think she was, though she'd freely admit she was a desperate one. The world she had been invited into, because of her situation and her good looks, had introduced her to an incredible lifestyle, and all she had to do was bring attractive street people and young tourists to a party, then have a good time.

What happened after that wasn't her responsibility.

That was the Operator and the bidders. Some of the people she brought in went home at the end of the night, with bidders uninterested. Others were snatched up within minutes, like the Americans last night. She didn't know what happened to them next. She didn't want to know, but she wasn't stupid. She tried to convince herself at first that these people she brought in were being kidnapped for ransom, but she had quickly dismissed that delusion.

Who paid ransom for street kids?

No, she had no doubt that every one of them she brought in and was bought at the auction were destined to be sex slaves or worse for the rest of their lives. But as long as nobody ever actually told her that, she could lie to herself to keep from going insane with guilt. It was why she had to get out. She had been planning to leave by the end of the year, but after last night's big score, she had enough to do it early. All she had to do was tough it out until the payment arrived, which wasn't until the cargo was delivered to the successful bidders.

She closed her eyes, squeezing them tight. It wasn't fair. None of it was fair. What she did day after day was despicable. Not only was it a crime, it was morally reprehensible and she hated herself more with each passing day, with each bonus, with each share of the take. But what choice did she have? She couldn't go home and face her stepbrother again. He'd be raping her the very first night. And she couldn't return to the streets. Girls like her were passed around far too often as the sexual playthings of alpha males who offered their protection in exchange for sexual favors that too often were reenactments of their own abuse.

It was a horrible, terrifying life, despite the brave face put on by those like her when offered help. Frequently the help put them into a system where they were abused again. It was a life not worth living, which is why many turned to drugs and alcohol to forget their suffering, and others simply cut out the middleman and killed themselves.

She had to get out, and as a few teenagers laughed as they boarded the same train car as her, she swore this was it. This was the end. Once she had her share deposited, she was disappearing, putting this life behind her once and for all. But she had to keep working for now, because if the payment was late, she'd still be expected to deliver for the next party.

She opened her eyes and spotted the four teenagers that had just boarded, one of whom she recognized from the streets.

Time to go to work.

Child Residence

Langley, Virginia

CIA Analyst Randy Child growled in frustration as his phone beeped yet again. He finally tore his eyes away from the screen as the epic game of Call of Duty continued on without him. His eyes narrowed when he saw the message from Sonya Tong.

Urgent you contact me immediately.

And that was two messages ago, the rest merely exclamation points.

He sighed. "RandyRandy97 AFK." He removed his headset, put down his controller, and grabbed his phone. He ran a greasy, cheese puff-stained finger across the screen and typed a quick message.

Sorry just saw this. What's up?

A link was sent.

Install this.

Child frowned. Normally he'd tell anybody who told him to install an app to go to hell, but this was Tong, a woman he had worked with since he first joined the Agency. He tapped the link, followed the instructions, and an app installed on his phone. A moment later, his phone vibrated in a different pattern than he had felt before and a message popped up on his screen.

Tap here to accept call.

It was definitely something bypassing the regular phone's interface. He tapped. "Hello?"

"Hi, Randy, it's Sonya. Do you have plans for the next two days?"

Child glanced at his game. "Sort of."

"Can you cancel them?"

"Why, do you need me to come in?"

"I need you to come in, but not to Langley. Listen carefully. You're about to be invited into the inner circle. If you don't want to be invited in, then say no now, because once you're in, you'll be privy to things that you can never speak about to anyone outside the circle, ever."

He gulped. He'd always suspected there was something going on. There was talk of a Chinese mole at the Agency. Could Tong be that mole? Was he about to get drawn into something that could see him go to prison for the rest of his life? But there was something else going on as well. In the operations center, Leroux and Tong far too often were privy to information that they shouldn't be. He was convinced they were getting private messages from Kane and other people. Could that be the inner circle she was talking about?

"I'm going to need more information. Just who's in this inner circle?"

There was a sound on the other end of the line then his eyes shot wide at the voice of his boss, Chris Leroux. "Randy, this is Chris. Do you want in or not?"

He squeezed his eyes shut, praying he wouldn't regret this. "I want in."

Medeci Fountain

Paris, France

Reading ended the call and uttered a string of curses that would make a sailor blush.

Humphrey giggled. "So, good news?"

He rolled his eyes at her. "Inspector Fontaine said she can't run the number without an investigation being opened, and a phone number pulled off the back of an invitation to a rave where no crime might have taken place other than trespassing, would never merit opening of said investigation."

"As much as I hate to say it, she's right."

Reading sighed. "I know, I know. Hopefully, we'll know soon enough, regardless."

"When did your friends indicate this new asset would be in place?"

"In about an hour."

Humphrey frowned. "It's really too bad we couldn't get them fully committed. It'd be a game changer."

Sasha finished off an apple juice. "Just who are these friends you keep talking about?"

"Like I said earlier, it's best not to ask questions."

Sasha chuckled. "Which is an answer in itself, isn't it? I'm guessing foreign intelligence. American, since they seem to be so interested in two missing Americans, so CIA."

Reading regarded him, not confirming or denying anything, simply letting the deductive process continue on its own.

"So, let's assume they are American intelligence, CIA. In order for them to officially get involved, this situation has to somehow affect the United States. A human trafficking ring, if that's indeed what's going on, isn't a threat to national security. But if American citizens are being kidnapped, especially well-connected American citizens, that would get them involved."

"You would hope the American government would get involved if their citizens were being kidnapped," agreed Reading, still not giving anything away.

"So as soon as we have proof that they were kidnapped, then the chains holding back your friends are removed."

"Hypothetically."

Sasha eyed him. "And money is no object?"

"No. Why?"

"If your friends' new asset can't get in place for an hour, I may know somebody who can help us right now."

"Who?"

"Someone I have come across while performing my duties as a guide. He lives in his mother's basement, he hasn't seen the light of day probably in three years, his hygiene is questionable, but he has no scruples about who he works for, doesn't ask any inappropriate questions, and we can be there in ten minutes if you give the word."

"It's given."

Sasha smiled, putting the car in gear. "Just one thing."

"What's that?"

"Don't tell him money is no object. Just offer him ten thousand euros, and you'll avoid all the haggling."

Humphrey leaned forward between the seats. "And what's your cut?"

Sasha laughed as he pulled out into traffic. "I can guarantee you it's not fifteen percent."

"Ten?"

"Fair, I think, don't you?"

Reading dialed Acton. "I don't give a shit how the money's divvied up if it gets us results."

Outside the Château

Paris, France

October 13, 1898

Leblanc stared at the château. In the light of day, it was an impressive display of wealth, belonging to a family who had made their fortune in shipping. They were once extremely wealthy, and the older generation had been the toast of the town. But the family had become rather reclusive after the son apparently married his first cousin, giving birth to twins that polite society only spoke of in whispers.

Jacques' father had perhaps described it best. "When the twins were born and everything appeared normal, you could hear the collective sigh from that château. But as they grew, it became quite clear they had problems, and the parents kept them locked away. I don't believe they've been seen for at least ten or fifteen years."

Archambault regarded the château from their carriage window. "I've always admired this place every time I passed it, but now that I know what's going on behind those walls, it gives me the shivers."

Leblanc agreed with his partner. On a sunny summer day, it was a breathtaking sight. But today, a damp dreary early October simply made the architectural elements appear sinister. Whatever was behind those walls wasn't joyous as one might expect from the home of one of Paris' most wealthy families.

"Are we going in?"

"No."

"Why not? Jacques could still be alive in there."

"He might be, but one doesn't go and just enter the home of a family like this unless one is absolutely sure of what they're going to find."

Archambault stared at him incredulously. "And you're not sure?"

Leblanc signaled for the coachman to drive on before replying. "While I have no doubt this is how and where our murderer is choosing his victims, I would have to assume that either he's taking them from here to do his dirty work, or has a place so well hidden that it might take us days or weeks to find it in a place this size. The pressure the family would put on the commissioner would put an end to any search quite quickly. We need to see him in action and find out who his partner is."

Archambault stared at him. "Partner? What partner?"

"The girl."

Archambault's eyes narrowed. "What girl?"

"The one that lured Jacques away from his friends. Think about it. A girl that none of them recognized, despite there only being members of high society at this party. A girl of the type of character that would walk up to some random young man and kiss him. She doesn't fit the guest list."

Archambault shrugged. "I don't see why not. Just because you're a member of high society doesn't mean you can't be promiscuous."

"True, but remember, she dragged him off and kept him away. For him to remain with her, from all accounts, was out of character. He should have turned around even if he was momentarily overcome, but he never did. He never left that party because he never had the option. Even if we ignore my idea that she's the partner, she likely is the last person to have seen him alive. We need to find her and question her. Give me five minutes with her and I'll know whether she's involved."

"How do you propose to find her?"

"I propose that you and the others return to the party next weekend with a sketch-artist drawing of the woman. Find her, and I think she'll lead us to our killer and we might just save another victim."

Paris–Le Bourget Airport

Paris, France

Present Day

Acton stepped off their Gulfstream G700, one of the fastest business jets on the market, and onto the tarmac, the early evening hour having taken a little bit of the edge off the heat radiating from the surface. He extended a hand and helped Laura down, then the two of them headed directly for the charter terminal, the airport staff already retrieving their luggage.

Progress was being made, but too much time had passed. Another CIA resource was being brought online and he was almost in position, but apparently Reading's guide provided by their travel agent knew someone who could get the job done. The mission was to find Bridgette to figure out what she knew. First, they had to confirm that Tommy and Mai had indeed been kidnapped. He had no doubt anymore. It had been too long, but they needed to hear the words, they needed to record the words so they could get the full resources of the American government on the case.

Then they needed to know who was behind it and where Tommy and Mai were being taken. Unfortunately, if Bridgette was indeed someone from the streets, she likely had no idea who was behind this, nor where they would be taken. While he feared she might know little that could help them today, she was on the inside, and if they could turn her or force her to help them, she might put them together with those who knew what was going on.

At least it was a lead.

They cleared customs, a mere formality for the well-heeled that used private jets, and were soon in their rental heading for their hotel, the GPS preprogrammed with their destination. Laura drove, the better driver between the two of them but also more familiar with the alien European traffic signs.

He glanced at her knuckles, white from gripping the steering wheel so hard. "Take a breath."

She flinched but did as told, flexing her fingers as she did so.

"You have to calm down. We need to think clearly if we're going to help them."

"If I get my hands on this Bridgette, I'm going to beat her within an inch of her life before I ask the first question."

Acton smiled slightly, having no doubt she was capable of doing exactly what she said. "As much as I'd like to see that, we might need her cooperation, because I doubt a street kid has been entrusted with the details we need. We're going to need her to lead us to those who do know, and if she shows up beaten to a bloody pulp, they're going to know something's wrong."

"You're right. But if something happens to them, I'm going on a killing spree."

Acton leaned over and squeezed her thigh. "You and me both."

CyberRat98's Residence

Paris, France

The ten-thousand-euro offer had been eagerly accepted and Reading had a sense the greasy hacker they were now dealing with would have done it for a thousand, but a one-hundred-euro commission for Sasha apparently wasn't enough. It didn't matter so long as it yielded results. His friends were footing the bill and they would have paid ten times that if it meant saving Tommy and Mai.

CyberRat98, as Sasha had called him, thrust his arms in the air in victory.

"What is it?" asked Reading.

"I'm in." CyberRat98 held up his hand. "Give me the number."

Humphrey handed over the number she had jotted on her notepad earlier, none of them willing to hand a phone over to a hacker they couldn't trust despite Sasha's assurances he was a white hat. CyberRat98 entered the number and after a few keystrokes and clicks, pointed at a large display to the right. A map of Paris appeared followed by scores of dots.

"What are we looking at?" asked Reading.

"Every place she received or sent a phone call or text message. It looks like the phone was activated last Sunday, then hasn't been used since around midnight last night. This is definitely a burner, prepaid, probably cash, no way to trace the owner."

"Can you give us a list of every phone number that's interacted with it? Also, if possible, who those numbers belong to?"

"Sure."

More activity, the fingers flying across the keyboard faster than Reading had ever seen. A paper spit out of a printer nearby. "There you go."

Reading retrieved the paper and skipped to the last few numbers, smacking the page as he handed it over to Humphrey. "The second last number is an incoming call from Tommy's phone."

"Well, if there was ever any doubt, it's gone now. She was their point of contact."

Reading turned toward the large display with the map. "What does this tell us?" he asked, unfamiliar with the city.

Sasha ran his finger along a line where most of the interactions had taken place. "This fits in with what we know about her. She likes to ride the Métro and this follows one of the main lines."

"All right, we need to get access to some surveillance footage from the Métro that matches up with the time of these calls. Do you think you can do that?"

CyberRat98 shrugged. "Sure, but it'll take some time, especially going through the footage. But you paid me for twenty-four hours of service, so you'll get it." He batted a hand over his shoulder as he turned back to his keyboard. "But get out of here before my mother gets upset. She doesn't like it when I have house guests. Sasha, I'll contact you when I get a face."

As if on cue, a shrill voice shouted something down the stairs and Reading cringed, as did Humphrey. Sasha laughed and turned to them. "All right, we better get out of here before she beats us with a broomstick."

Ritz Paris

Paris, France

The hotel suite they were in had been specifically chosen by their travel agent to be a base of operations while they were in Paris. It had a separate bedroom and a large living area with a dining table that would double as a conference table, along with a hardwired gigabit line. Acton set up their gear as Laura freshened up, and he soon had their Wi-Fi router connected to the highspeed Internet and several laptops opened up on the table.

He brought up his email and quickly went through it then checked his limited social media for anything from Tommy or Mai, and as expected, came up empty. He was already up to date on his phone messages, Reading having just sent one indicating they had made some progress. He and Humphrey, along with their guide, were on their way here now. There was nothing new from Kane's end except that Randy Child had arrived, so they now had two skilled hackers working the problem.

Laura emerged from the bedroom. "All yours. Anything new?"

"Nothing except that Randy Child has arrived." Acton stripped out of his clothes as Laura sat at the table, bringing up her own accounts on her laptop.

"Why do I get a sense this is going to be a whole lot of hurry up and wait?"

Acton chuckled as he headed into the bedroom, tossing his clothes on the bed, then into the bathroom. He started his business, leaving the door open so they could continue to talk. "Because we're working a case. Once we find this Bridgette character, something tells me we'll be run off our feet." There was a knock at the door and he cursed. "Um, can you close the bedroom door before you get that?"

Laura snickered. "This is what you get for being totally comfortable with your body."

He flushed the toilet. "Apparently not *totally* comfortable."

The door was closed and pleasantries were exchanged as Reading and Michelle arrived with their guide. He quickly completed his ablutions then donned fresh clothes before joining the others. "Hey, Hugh, Michelle. Good to see you again."

Reading was already sitting in a comfortable chair, looking exhausted. He flung a hand toward a man standing nearby. "This is Sasha, our guide."

Acton shook the man's hand. "Nice to meet you. Any word from our hacker friend?"

"Not yet, but he says he's in the system. It's only a matter of time."

"Good. We need to find this woman, the sooner the better. It's almost eight, which means they could be twenty hours away from here by now."

Laura frowned as she retrieved bottles of water from the fridge for everyone. "That means they could be anywhere in the world."

"If they went by plane," said Humphrey. "Which I doubt they would."

"Why's that?"

"It would have the most security. They'd likely transport by private vehicle."

Laura handed out the bottles of water, passing one of them to Acton.

"How far could they have gotten by now?" he asked.

Reading shrugged as he took a long swig of his water. "It depends on when they started, but even the most conservative estimate would be that they've been traveling for at least twelve hours."

"Getting out of Paris would eat up about an hour of that," said Sasha, "but then it would be pretty smooth sailing. They could absolutely be out of the country by now."

"Where would they take them?" Laura sat. "I mean, if they are being trafficked, where do those people go?"

"Anywhere in the world." Reading finished his water and Humphrey waved off Laura as she rose to get another bottle for him. "We have to assume they're being sold into the sex trade."

Laura cried out involuntarily and Acton took her hand, as equally appalled at hearing Reading say what they had always suspected.

"Now, that can mean anywhere in the world from Moscow to Berlin to Washington to New York. Anywhere, but most likely the Middle East."

Humphrey handed him a fresh bottle of water. "Yes. Now, the one advantage Tommy and Mai would have if they did end up in a major city like that would be who they are. If they could escape, they could go to any police station or the American embassy and get help. Most of these girls that are pulled into this system are from poor countries in Africa and Asia, and they're told that if they try to escape or resist, their families back home will be targeted. Tommy and Mai are educated enough to see through those threats, but I have a feeling that that's not what's actually going on. This seems to be too sophisticated an operation to just be recruiting for the sex trade. Those girls are a dime a dozen in Southeast Asia and most of Africa. An operation as sophisticated as this makes me think the organizers are catering to a higher-end clientele."

"So, not the sex trade?" asked Laura, a hint of hope in her voice.

Humphrey frowned. "I'm sorry, but no, it would still be the sex trade, but likely they'll end up somewhere in the Middle East, servicing a wealthy sheik. We've worked cases where millions have been paid if very specific criteria are met."

"Millions?" Acton stared at her incredulously. "People actually pay millions?"

"Absolutely. But again, that's a sophisticated black market. Very sophisticated. And we don't know if these people are tied in with that. If they are, the good news would be that if someone just paid a million or more for them, they'll probably be treated with kid gloves until they're delivered."

"And you think it could be to the Middle East?"

"It's likely. Western citizens, especially Americans, are highly prized because they're hard to come by."

"Well, getting them to the Middle East doesn't sound easy. Yes, you could take them overland if you just look at a map and ignore the borders, but it can't be that simple."

Laura agreed. "James is right. Traveling within the Schengen Agreement area is relatively easy, but once you leave it, I would think things become a lot more difficult. To get into those areas like Saudi and the UAE, you're talking going through countries like Turkey, Syria, Iraq."

Humphrey shook her head. "No, I assume they would bypass those countries. My guess is they're heading for the Mediterranean, perhaps the Aegean. They'll transfer them to a boat then take them to North Africa where they probably have a network set up with all the right people bribed to look the other way. These operations can be very sophisticated. The question is, is this operation that sophisticated? The only way we're going to find that out is to locate this Bridgette girl."

Reading cleared his throat and Acton regarded him. His old friend was still not back to his normal self though he did appear far better than he had just a couple of weeks ago. This kind of stress and exertion, however, couldn't be good for him, though he didn't dare say anything as that would just piss him off. "We do have some info on that, if Nutbar-twenty-seven, or whatever the hell his name was, is as good at his job as Sasha says."

Sasha leaned in. "CyberRat98."

Reading grunted. "Same shit, different flies." He handed over a printout that he retrieved from his inner pocket. Laura took it. "These are all the numbers that called or texted Bridgette's phone or that she called or texted. Look at the bottom, you're going to see Tommy's number there."

Laura scanned the pages then handed them over to Acton. "So that confirms what we already knew, that she was their point of contact."

Acton shook the pages. "These are all the calls? There aren't many."

Reading agreed. "It's most likely a burner. Looks like it was activated last Sunday and she stopped using it last night. She's most likely on a brand new one as of today, and it'll be tossed at the next rave."

Acton put the pages on the table. "Can we make any use of that? I mean, find a pattern?"

"We already did. It looks like the vast majority of the calls or messages occurred along a major Métro line. Her former friends said she likes to ride the rails and it appears she still does."

Laura leaned forward. "So then she could be on the Métro right now."

"She could be."

"Then I, for one, don't want to just sit here and wait. As soon as we found out about the phone, we were hoping to use it to track her, but now that we know it's been most likely disposed of, we've got nothing. We've got Dylan's team trying to find footage of her so that we can get a better shot of her face, but even if we get it, we still have to find her."

Sasha leaned in. "CyberRat is also trying to get footage from the subways to match up with the call history."

Laura acknowledged him with a brief look. "But even that only gives us her face. We still need to go out and find her. We've got a general description. We know where she likes to frequent. I say we go down to this subway line, split into two teams. Sasha, you stay with the vehicle, and we each board a train, search it, and if we see someone suspicious, call it in. If we don't, get off and get on the next one. We have to do something. I'm tired of just sitting here."

Reading rose. "Agreed. Sasha, you stay with the vehicle and try to keep up with us on street level. Laura, you'll come with me. Jim, you go with Michelle. That way, if something happens, each team has someone with police credentials, and hopefully soon either Asshat-Five-Nine or Dylan's team has a face for us."

Unknown Location

Mai lay in her bed, staring up at the ceiling, agonizing over the fact the man she loved was directly above her, less than three feet away. She wanted to communicate with him somehow but had no clue how to accomplish that. She had no doubt he was worried about her, and she just wanted to let him know she was alive and nearby. When she had first woken up, she had kicked and screamed and had heard no response. Surely, Tommy would have done the same, and she had heard nothing in her entire time in this prison.

It had to mean the pods they were in were extremely well-insulated, or perhaps when Tommy had awoken, she was still passed out and didn't hear him, and then he was too scared to do anything when he heard her. She had to assume that if he did hear her initial reaction, he didn't hear her voice. He might have been too scared to respond to a ruckus from a stranger. She reached up and tapped three times. She turned her head to the side to listen for a response but heard nothing. She tapped again, this time harder, praying for any response, and her heart leaped as three knocks were returned.

She had established communication with the love of her life. Now the question was, how could they take advantage of it?

The Château
Paris, France
October 22, 1898

Isabelle's knee bounced uncontrollably and Jacques wasn't there to calm her. The past two weeks had been unbearable but she had insisted on coming, as had all her friends. They were determined to find justice for not only Jacques, but Pierre as well, and the other victims of this madman. She had never seen the girl in question, but she was certain she would recognize the type.

Archambault was with them, young enough to pass as a party goer and wearing finery provided by Richard so he would fit in. "Now, you've all seen the sketch, and you two"—he indicated Richard and Guy—"have actually seen her. I want you two splitting up. I don't want the only eyes that have seen her in the same part of the room. Now remember, if she's not part of society and she is in on this, she's most likely alone. Now alone doesn't mean she's standing by herself. She could be at the periphery of a group, making it appear as if she's part of it, but not. If

162

she's chosen the next victim, then she might already be with a man. Don't focus too much on the description of her clothing from last time. She might be wearing something completely different. She could have changed the color of her hair, anything. Focus on the eyes and the mouth, but also focus on the mannerisms.

"When we get there, we'll split up. We'll each make a circuit of the reception hall, then meet back near the entrance. Nobody leaves the ballroom under any circumstances, even if you see her. You come find me and then I pursue." He held up a whistle, Leblanc having given them all one. "If there's any trouble, blow on your whistle and keep blowing. I don't want any more victims tonight." He grinned. "Too much paperwork."

Isabelle was in no mood for jokes and merely responded with a weak smile. The carriage came to a halt and Archambault blew out the candle, plunging them into darkness. The door opened and she was helped out by a footman. The rest followed, and as they climbed the steps into what she was certain was the killer's lair where Jacques had taken his final breath, her heart raced faster than it ever had.

Caroline took her hand and squeezed, snapping her back to reality. "Breathe, my dear, breathe."

She inhaled deeply through her nose then exhaled slowly, repeating the process as she struggled to regain control.

"Just remember why we're here," said Caroline. "We're here for Jacques and Pierre. We have to stay calm so that we can find their killers and let them rest in peace."

They passed through the doors and everything appeared almost identical to last time, yet it was different. The music that had consumed her two weeks ago was but a dull thud in the background. The jubilant party goers moved as if in slow motion, everything a caricature of real life, as if all were putting on a show just for her. Their laughter, their celebrations, merely a put-on hiding the miseries they all suffered from, as if they all knew this was merely a front for something evil.

Who was giving the parties and why? It was a question she hadn't really been interested in getting an answer to last time, but it was the ultimate question, wasn't it? When one is invited to a party, one should naturally ask who the host is and question why, throughout the event, they never made an appearance. It was so obvious now that she knew what it was all about, but why wasn't it to all these others blissfully ignorant to the danger that walked among them?

Caroline squeezed her hand again. "Are you going to be all right?"

"Yes, I'm fine now. Let's just get this over with."

The six of them split up. She had the image of the girl burned in her mind, yet would she recognize her among the huge crowd? She stared blindly at the revelers and how ridiculous they all appeared, merely there to make sure they were seen by those they felt mattered. They were all fools, just as she had been. Everyone wanted to be seen at the most exclusive ticket in town, to partake in some stranger's food and drink, to dance to his imported music.

She stopped as she realized she wasn't doing her job. Rather than searching for the woman who might have lured Jacques away to be killed, she was instead judging those she had grown up with. She sniffed hard, bracing herself, her entire being on the razor's edge of collapsing into a puddle of tears. She had to keep it together. Jacques was dead. Pierre was dead. So were two others. And if she didn't do her job properly, a fifth person could die tonight.

She stood off to the side and slowly scanned the room from left to right, dismissing anyone she recognized, focusing instead on any women standing alone or any that were just couples. It was much earlier in the evening than when Jacques had been led off by the woman they were searching for, and she was doubtful that a new target would have been picked already. She was quite certain that alcohol had played a factor. A sober Jacques would have never gone with her, but a drunk Jacques would have played along for the fun of it.

After all, he had no girlfriend.

Her chest ached and she squeezed her hands, her fingernails biting into her palms as she struggled to regain control. She inhaled deeply then exhaled slowly.

"Isabelle!"

She spun toward the voice and suppressed a frown at the sight of a classmate, Sophie, rushing toward her, a pout on her lips as her arms extended for a hug. "I'm so sorry to hear about Jacques."

Despite best efforts, the story had gotten out, much to the annoyance of everyone involved.

Sophie embraced her, hugging her hard. "You must be absolutely devastated."

Isabelle extricated herself politely and Sophie held her by both shoulders, staring into her eyes.

"But perhaps not so much so, huh? After all, you're here and it's only been two weeks." Sophie frowned. "You know, I always thought you two would end up together." Her eyes narrowed and her head tilted slightly. "Did you two have a fight that night? When I saw him with that other girl, I was gobsmacked. I couldn't believe he would do that to you, but if you had a fight—"

Isabelle cut her off. "You saw the girl?"

"Yes, we all did. If we hadn't heard the next day that he was missing and presumed dead, I'm sure it would be the talk of the town."

Isabelle grabbed Sophie's arm, stopping her once again. "This girl, do you know her? Do the others know who she is?"

"No."

"Do any of you know?"

Another headshake. "No, none of us recognized her, but none of that matters now, does it? There's no point being jealous of a last-minute fling."

"It has nothing to do with that. If you see her again, let me know. It's extremely important."

Sophie stared at her. "What's going on?"

"Nothing I can talk about. Just if you see her, if any of you see her, find me."

Sophie shook her head. "There's no need."

"What do you mean?"

Sophie pointed behind Isabelle. "She's right over there."

Isabelle spun toward where Sophie was pointing and her heart leaped into her throat at the sight of the girl, exactly as described by Richard and

166

Guy, standing next to a group of people that Isabelle recognized, sipping a cocktail as she slowly swayed to the music. The woman's head turned toward Isabelle and she looked away, once again facing Sophie. "I need you to find Richard and Guy and bring them here right away."

"Why?"

"Please just do it. Find them!"

"All right, all right, I'll go get them."

Sophie left, leaving Isabelle alone, and as she stood there in her own void on the floor, she felt dangerously exposed. She glanced out of the corner of her eye for the woman that might have killed Jacques and found her still near the group she had attached herself to, but not looking in her direction. Isabelle drifted over to another group of people she didn't recognize and stood next to them, her back to most of them so they wouldn't interact with her.

She risked a glance over at the woman and gasped when she wasn't where she had last seen her. She searched the crowd and spotted her walking toward the same hallway Jacques had been lured down. She couldn't risk losing her. She searched for the others but couldn't see them. She gripped the whistle she had been holding the entire time, meant for an emergency, but was this an emergency? Finding the woman had always been a long shot, but wasn't it critical that they catch her rather than simply say she was there?

She pressed the whistle to her lips then stopped. Archambault had said they were certain it was a man committing the murders, that this woman was his partner, that overpowering, murdering, decapitating, then disposing of the body was simply too much for one woman to have carried out. And she agreed after having seen how slight of frame the seductress was. If she blew the whistle, they might catch the girl, but she might never reveal who her partner was.

And Isabelle wanted justice.

Archambault had told them during the carriage ride here that the coroner believed the same night the next victim was taken, the body of the previous was disposed of. It could mean that Jacques was here. She'd given up all hope that he was alive, but at least he might receive a decent burial and be able to rest in peace. She lowered the whistle and instead made a beeline for the hallway, her pulse pounding in her ears as her rational mind told her to stop. But she was committed now.

She was determined to get justice for the man who was to be her husband.

The Métro

Paris, France

Present Day

Reading was laboring. It would have been a non-stop day for him, and the poor dear must be exhausted. Laura regarded him as they boarded the second subway, the first having proven a bust. "Why don't you just sit here and I'll check to see if she's here."

"No, we stick together."

She placed her hand on her friend's chest. "You're tired. There's no shame in that, and you know I can take care of myself. We're dealing with a teenage girl."

"Who might be armed and you're not."

"If she's armed, I'll disarm her." She pulled out her phone. "I'll call you and I'll be on the line with you the entire time."

He frowned but acquiesced, which told her he was exhausted. The Hugh Reading she knew would never let her go alone. "Don't confront her."

She patted him on the shoulder and dialed his number. He answered the call, pressing the phone to his ear as she did the same.

"If you see anything you tell me and I'll join you."

"I promise." She gave another cursory scan to the car they were in then headed to the next one. There were so many young women that matched the general description that it was easy to give up hope, yet this was all she had. She couldn't just sit in a hotel room praying for a lucky break. This was Mai, this was Tommy. She had to be doing something, otherwise she'd go mad with worry.

She moved on to the next car and found much of the same.

"Anything?" asked Reading.

"I'm in the third car now. Nothing so far." She slowly made her way down the aisle, her eyes rapidly scanning and dismissing the passengers. She turned her head to the right to examine the next row and caught a young woman staring directly at her. Laura diverted her eyes to the woman's lap, a cellphone held loosely by a PopSocket gripped by two fingers.

And Laura gasped.

One of the fingers had Mai's ring on it.

"What is it?" asked Reading.

"I found her. She has Mai's ring."

Bridgette leaped to her feet and Laura shoved her back in the seat, activating the camera on her phone and taking a picture.

"Let me go, you crazy bitch!" shouted the girl in French.

"I'm coming toward you now," said Reading.

"Help me! She's trying to rob me!"

Several passengers took notice and two men rose, approaching her. Laura pointed at them, speaking in fluent French. "Stand back! This woman is wanted for questioning in a kidnapping."

"You're police?"

"No, but my friend is. He'll be here in a moment."

"Then you don't have any right to stop her."

Laura pointed at Bridgette's hand. "She has my friend's ring. She stole that from her when she kidnapped her."

Bridgette held the ring up. "It's mine, I swear! She's trying to steal it!" She tried to stand again and Laura shoved her back into the seat. The two men rushed forward, reaching for Laura. Laura shoved her phone in her pocket then took a fighting stance. The two men exchanged looks and laughed.

"Equal rights, lady. You want to fight like a man, we'll treat you like a man." The talker advanced and her foot darted out, crushing his balls. He doubled over in agony as Bridgette darted out of her seat. Laura cursed, reaching for her, but the girl evaded her grasp as the second man stepped over his downed partner. The subway slowed for its next stop and Bridgette pressed against the doors. If they didn't catch her now, they might never find her. She'd go underground and never get on the train again, especially now that they had her picture.

"I don't have time for this," muttered Laura as the train came to a halt. She dodged to the left as he swung with his right, then she raised her right foot and kicked, snapping his knee, as it was now clearly self-defense. He crumpled to the floor in agony as the doors opened.

Bridgette squeezed through, sprinting out of sight. Laura bolted after her, fishing her phone out of her pocket as the two overly zealous good Samaritans writhed in agony behind her. She spotted Bridgette racing up an escalator, shoving people out of her way, screaming, "Help me! Help me! She's crazy!"

Laura pressed her phone to her ear to hear Reading shouting, "Laura, are you there?"

"Yes, I'm all right. Get off the train."

"What?"

"Get off the train. We're not on it anymore."

Reading cursed and she glanced over her shoulder as she reached the stairs and spotted him squeezing through the doors just as they closed. They made brief eye contact and she took the nearly empty stairs two at a time as Bridgette reached the top of the escalator.

"Take the escalator," she told Reading. "You'll explode that heart if you take the stairs."

"Bloody hell, I'm too old for this shit."

She laughed as her legs burned from the physical exertion. "That's why you took the desk job."

"Bollocks. I took the desk job because you and your husband made me too public a figure."

She reached the top of the steps and sprinted toward the doors, following the commotion Bridgette had left behind.

"I'd tell you to be careful, but you've ignored every single thing I've said so far."

She pushed through the doors, emerging outside into the cool evening.

And smiled.

Bridgette didn't know who the woman was chasing her, but she definitely had training. She had only seen moves like that in the movies, and it had her wondering if she was more than a friend of Tommy and Mai's. She pressed her thumb against the ring as she sprinted down the street. She shouldn't have taken it, but she couldn't resist. It was so beautiful, especially for a piece of costume jewelry.

But now she had to wonder, was it just cheap metal and paste? Her pursuer had recognized it immediately, and paste jewelry wasn't something you showed off to friends. If it was real, it had to be worth a fortune, and if a young girl like Mai was wearing it, it had to mean Tommy's family was very wealthy, and that could pose a problem. She had to warn her employers, but she had no way of reaching them. None of them were given any contact information so that if they were arrested, they couldn't cut a deal to betray those behind the network.

There was only one person she could think of to call. She ducked in an alleyway and dialed his number. As it rang, a foot scraped behind her. Someone grabbed her and she cried out, her phone clattering to the ground as she struggled to break the iron grip of the arm wrapped around her neck. The woman was impossibly strong. As the pressure increased on her neck she began to black out, and as she scratched at her pursuer's arm, her eyes narrowed, puzzled at how hairy it was.

Laura hopped in the back seat of the SUV and Sasha started the engine before handing her several zip ties.

"Wrists and ankles."

Laura didn't bother asking why the man had zip ties on him or how he had managed to not only reach the station but capture, incapacitate, and load Bridgette into the back of the SUV so quickly. She secured Bridgette's hands then as she bent down to secure the woman's feet, the passenger door opened and the SUV rocked.

"Bloody hell. How did you get here so fast?"

Sasha laughed. "It helps if you know the city like the back of your hand, but the key is that traffic is fairly light at this time of night."

Reading dialed his phone. "Jim, it's Hugh. We've got her. Where are you?"

Laura finished binding Bridgette's ankles then sat up as Reading relayed her husband's location.

Sasha put the car in gear. "That's just one stop ahead. Tell him we'll be there in five minutes."

Reading passed on the ETA then ended the call. He turned in his seat and looked their prisoner up and down. "So, this is her?"

Laura nodded. "Yes."

"You're sure?"

Laura removed the ring and held it up. "This is Mai's engagement ring. There's no doubt about it. This is her."

Reading pulled an evidence bag from his inner pocket and opened it. "Put that in here."

Laura dropped it inside and he sealed it then signed it, adding the date and time. He put it in his inner pocket. "This is our first piece of solid evidence. This is proof a crime was committed. We still don't know what the crime is, but we at least have her on theft."

Sasha picked a phone out of the cupholder. "This is hers. She was making a call when I took her down."

Laura eyed him. "Just what did you do to her? She's out cold."

"Sleeper hold. She'll be awake in a couple of minutes." He pointed at the glove compartment. "There's a balaclava in there, just in case our guest decides to get noisy."

Reading retrieved it and handed it back to Laura. He regarded Sasha. "You're not just a guide, are you?"

Sasha chuckled. "A man's allowed to have a side hustle, isn't he?"

"I'm guessing ex-Special Forces."

Sasha grinned. "And I'm not entertaining any guesses. I was hired as a guide and all I did was guide a woman you were interested in into my vehicle."

Bridgette moaned and her eyes fluttered open, and after a moment of disorientation, she gasped and jerked away from Laura, pressing into the corner of the back seat. "What the hell's going on?" She noticed her hands and ankles were bound and the fear on her face grew.

And Laura had no sympathy for her, none whatsoever, because her fear couldn't compare to that now gripping Tommy and Mai. "Shut up," said Laura in English, and Bridgette flinched, her mouth snapping closed. "Your name is Bridgette. What's your last name?"

The girl said nothing.

"No problem. We'll just run your prints. I have no doubt you're in the system," said Reading.

Laura glared at her. "Where are my friends Tommy and Mai?"

"I don't know who you're talking about."

"Bullshit. You know exactly who I'm talking about. Tommy and Mai." Laura pulled up their photos on her phone and shoved it in Bridgette's face. "We've got video of you with them last night. Now, what the hell happened to them? Where are they?"

Bridgette's jaw clenched and she turned away. Laura's hand darted out and gripped the woman by the chin, twisting her head to face her.

"If anything happens to them, I'll see to it that the rest of your short life is filled with nothing but horror and pain."

Bridgette stared at her, tears filling her eyes. "They'll kill me."

Laura relaxed her grip slightly. "Who's they?"

Bridgette shrugged. "I don't know. Nobody ever uses names. I'm a nobody. I just bring them in."

"Bring them in to what?"

"The auction."

Bile filled Laura's mouth and her stomach churned at the word. It confirmed her worst fears, but she had to hear the words from the woman's mouth. "What do you mean by auction?"

"Video from the party is shown on the dark web. Bidders from around the world indicate who they're interested in, then the bidding begins. When a winner is declared, that person is removed from the party and prepared for transport. Anyone who isn't bid on goes home at the end of the night."

Reading leaned closer. "How many are you taking each night?"

Bridgette shrugged. "It varies."

"How many last night?"

"Ten."

"Including Tommy and Mai?"

Bridgette nodded.

"And where are they taken?"

"I have no idea. I only know what I know because I got friendly with one of the people involved in the auction."

Sasha came to a stop and James and Humphrey joined them in the rear row. Bridgette's eyes widened as those opposing her grew in number.

Reading held up Bridgette's phone. "Who were you trying to call?"

Bridgette stared at her bound hands. "They'll kill me."

James reached forward, placing a single finger on Bridgette's chin and lifting it so he could stare her in the eyes. "I love Mai as if she were my daughter. If anything happens to her, you're going to wish you were dead. Now, answer the question."

Bridgette's entire body trembled and the tears flowed, her eyes wide with terror. "It's Victor. I was trying to call Victor. He's the only one I know that's involved with the auction. I thought maybe he might know who was involved so that I could warn them about you. I'm sorry about your friends, but I had no choice. Once you're in, you're in, it's impossible to get out. I've been saving money for over a year now. I was planning on leaving this weekend, I swear. I've got a passport, ID, a whole new identity. I'm going to Canada to try to make up for what I've done."

Laura glared at her. "Do you really think there's any way you can make up for selling innocent boys and girls into sexual slavery?"

Bridgette shook her head. "No, there isn't, you're right. I deserve whatever happens to me, just don't hand me over to them. People are bidding on me all the time. According to Victor, the only reason I haven't been sold is because I bring in more than the bids for me. That's why I'm leaving, because one of these days the bid for me is going to be too high to pass up and then I'll be sold, just like the others. Please don't do that to me."

James grunted. "You didn't seem to have a problem condemning Tommy and Mai and countless others to the same fate, so I don't see why we should be doing you any favors."

Laura played along, knowing full well no matter how angry they were, her husband would never condemn even the guilty to a life of sexual slavery. "If you help us, then we'll help you, but you have to tell us everything, and I mean everything. Every little detail, no matter how much it incriminates you, no matter how much it puts you at risk, you tell us every single thing you know and we'll help you."

Bridgette stared at her, wiping the tears from her eyes. "How can you help me? These people are powerful, they're dangerous, they're evil. How can you possibly help me?"

Laura smiled slightly. "How do you think we found you?"

Bridgette stared at her. "What do you mean?"

"I mean, our friends haven't even been gone twenty-four hours and yet we already found you. How do you think that's possible?"

Bridgette's eyes narrowed as she thought. "I don't know," she finally said.

"And you don't need to know, but if we can find you in less than a day, that should indicate to you how well-connected we are and what resources we have access to. Now, do we have a deal?"

Bridgette's eyes flitted around the SUV, making brief eye contact with everyone staring at her, then her shoulders slumped. "Yes."

Unknown Location

Tears flowed freely as Mai listened to the tapping repeated back to her. She had been struggling for a way to convey to Tommy that it was her, but neither of them knew Morse code, and all they could do was tap a certain number of times back and have it repeated. Then an idea had struck her and she had tapped out a tune, a tune that she hoped he would recognize. It was the pattern of the opening sequence of his podcast. Mission Impossible. There had been no response the first time. The second time, however, it had been repeated back perfectly, and it was followed by half a dozen excited knocks.

He knew it was her.

He was indeed a few feet away and he was alive. Now the question was, how could they escape? All they had established was that each other was there. There was no way they could coordinate any type of effort to escape.

She knocked hard on the outer panel and it opened a few moments later. "I need to use the bathroom."

"I told you not to drink all that water."

She shrugged. "I was thirsty. Blame whatever you guys gave me last night."

He beckoned her out and she climbed down. She headed slowly for the bathroom, her eyes wandering about the narrow confines. This time she took note of the handles on the prison doors. They were simple latches, pull up and out, and the door would open. There was no evidence that any type of key was required. She grabbed a Gatorade bottle off the food table then entered the bathroom and closed the door. She sat on the toilet to do her business and opened her bottle, squirting a blast of the sweet electrolyte-laden fluid into her mouth.

Her eyes roamed every square inch for something, anything that could be used as a weapon, but she found nothing. He outweighed her two to one. There was no way she could overpower him, even if she got in a lucky hit. She needed help and there was only one thing she could think of to do. She stopped peeing and emptied her Gatorade bottle into the sink. She positioned it and resumed peeing, filling it about a quarter of the way. She wiped then flushed the toilet, filling the bottle back up to the top with water from the sink, then screwed the squirt-cap back in place.

She drew a deep breath. What she was about to try was insane and had little chance of succeeding, but she didn't care. She had to try something, and if she died doing it, that was fine by her.

Anything was better than the alternative.

She inhaled deeply but it didn't help steady her hammering heart. These could be the final moments of her life, a life in which she had accomplished so little. She was too young to die. She was supposed to marry Tommy, have children, and grow old together.

And that was what she was fighting for. She was fighting for her future, for those children yet to be born.

She glanced at herself in the mirror, saddened that she was so small compared to her opponent. She had to act swiftly and without hesitation if she had any chance of succeeding. She drew another breath and clenched her jaw, nodding at herself.

You can do this.

She opened the door, her Gatorade bottle gripped in her left hand.

"What took you so long?" asked the Caretaker.

"Number two," she said as she walked toward him. She reached the first pair of prison cells and her pulse pounded in her ears as she trembled.

Do it!

Her hand darted out, grabbing the top handle. She pulled and the entire side of the pod lifted as she was already reaching for the handle of the one below.

"What the hell do you think you're doing?"

She ignored him. "Get out! We have to fight!" she yelled, opening the second pod then rushing forward. The Caretaker charged toward her and she raised her bottle, squeezing it in his face as she opened a third pod. "Get out and fight! Get out and fight! It's our only chance!"

"What the hell's in that?" cried the Caretaker, spitting as she sprayed more at his face and opened a fourth pod as somebody stumbled out behind her.

"Fight him! Come on, everybody! Get out and fight!" She reached Tommy's pod and yanked on the handle, spraying the last of her improvised chemical weapon at their captor. Tommy stared at her, startled. "Get out and fight!"

He jumped out, his head swiveling to take in his surroundings, then he spotted the Caretaker charging toward them, once again enraged at her actions.

Tommy rushed toward him and grabbed him, but the love of her life was easily fifty pounds lighter than his opponent and had never been very physical. Someone else rushed past her, then another, joining Tommy in the fray. She took the opportunity to open the rest of the compartments, finding the last two empty.

They were ten against one. They were going to win.

After a few minutes of struggle, four of them had the man pinned to the ground, everyone gasping from the effort.

"Find something to tie him up with," said Mai, looking about.

"I don't see anything," said Tommy.

"Sheets from the bed! Pillowcases!" shouted someone.

Mai reached into one of the pods and grabbed a pillow, pulling it from its case. She tossed the pillowcase toward the group then grabbed another, tossing a second over, and within moments they had his wrists and ankles bound.

Everyone backed off, chests heaving, nobody yet noticing that they were all naked. Tommy came over and hugged her.

"Are you all right?"

"I am now, but this isn't over."

183

"No, it's not." He turned to the group. "Does anybody know what's going on? Why we were taken?"

Head shakes and a few translations into French was the response.

Mai grabbed the sheet from her pod and wrapped it around her, everyone rapidly following suit.

"Well, obviously we were all taken against our will," said someone. "The last thing I remember was being at the party. Somebody handed me a drink and then I don't remember much after that."

Everyone in the room expressed similar recollections. One of the girls turned to Mai. "What do we do now?"

Mai gulped as everyone faced her as if she were the leader, and perhaps she was. She had, after all, effected their escape. "We need to search this place top to bottom and see what supplies we have. We need to find weapons, things to fight back with." She pointed at the rear. "We need to figure out how to open that door."

"Sorry, sweetheart, but it needs a code and only I have it," laughed the Caretaker.

The other boy turned to her. "I'll make him talk."

She didn't agree with torture, but this man was delivering them to a lifetime of just that. She nodded. "Do whatever it takes. We need that code." The boy took a knee then punched the man in the face repeatedly. Mai looked away. "All right, let's start searching."

Tommy cocked an ear. "What's that?"

She couldn't hear anything over the pulse pounding in her ears. "What's what?"

"A hissing sound."

Everyone stopped what they were doing and listened. Mai smelled something and gasped. "They're gassing us!"

Victor's Residence

Paris, France

Victor clinked his wine glass with Cheryl's. She had turned out to be a delight, one of the better pieces of trash he had picked up off the floor after the raves. His idea of a good time with these girls was likely not what most expected. When they woke up, he told them a story of how he had rescued them from some pig that had drugged them, then offered them sanctuary. He'd wine them, dine them, show them a life most had never seen or thought they would ever see again.

Most were receptive. He was a good-looking guy, lived in a fancy apartment, and once the booze and drugs came out, they willingly gave themselves to him. And then they would play house, boyfriend and girlfriend, with the understanding that once one got sick of the other it was over. It never lasted more than a week or two. Quite often it only lasted a day, but it was a little bit of normalcy in his life that he couldn't otherwise have. The game he was involved in was simply too dangerous to fall in love with somebody and bring them inside. He had an exit plan, almost enough money saved to escape, an entirely new identity already created that he would use at the first hint anything was wrong.

Cheryl put her glass down and straddled him. "Now, how can I thank you for saving me?"

He smirked. "I can think of a few ways."

She dropped onto the floor and reached for his belt. "So can I."

There was a knock at the door and he cursed.

"Expecting someone?"

"No, I never get visitors."

"Then it must be important."

There was another knock and he growled. "I'd better get that. Something tells me they're not going away."

She pouted but backed off, and he rose with a rager that he hoped whoever he greeted didn't notice. He walked up to the door but didn't open it. "Who is it?"

"It's Bridgette. Let me in."

His eyebrows shot up. Bridgette had been here once before when she had first started. Wine, dinner, sex, the usual routine. She was using him to get information and he had no problem with that, but the agreement had been that it was a one-night event and she was to forget where he lived. For her to be here meant something had gone wrong.

She knocked again, this time louder. "Let me in!"

He cursed and turned back to Cheryl. "I'm sorry. It's a friend of mine from work. Do you mind waiting in the bedroom?"

Cheryl shrugged and left the room. The bedroom door clicked shut though he had no doubt an ear was pressed against it. He opened the door and his eyes bulged as Bridgette was pulled aside and three men, all larger than him, rushed in, two grabbing him by either arm and dragging him to the nearest chair as the other searched the apartment, quickly finding Cheryl and bringing her out into the living area. He was bound to the chair with zip ties while Bridgette was brought in by two women and pushed onto the couch with Cheryl.

The flurry of activity took barely a minute and he didn't bother protesting or shouting for help. These were either the people he worked for, rivals to those he worked for, or they had sold the wrong person at auction and these people were searching for them. Whoever they were, this wasn't good. He had done nothing wrong that should piss off his employers, but the same couldn't be said for the other two possibilities. He'd have to play his cards right, otherwise, he could find himself lying in a pool of his own blood in the next few minutes.

The youngest man took up position by the door. He was apparently the muscle. The oldest sat at the dining room table, slightly out of breath. The man who appeared to be in charge jerked his head toward Cheryl.

"Who's she?" asked the man in an American accent.

"Just a friend."

"Is she involved?"

"Involved in what?"

"Don't play stupid. Your friend Bridgette told us everything." The man held his phone out and Victor's eyes flared slightly as photos of the two Americans were shown. This was the risk with taking tourists. Sometimes they weren't who you thought they were. Street kids rarely had connections and were never missed, not in less than twenty-four hours of being taken. "Now we know they were sold at auction last night. You were involved in that auction."

"I don't know—"

The American slapped him hard, the sting causing Victor's eyes to water. He couldn't recall ever being slapped in his life. Punched, yes, but not slapped. The pain was different. It lasted longer and was accompanied by a sense of humiliation. "You keep lying to me and I'll set him loose on you." The man pointed to the guard at the door who sneered as if eager to start breaking body parts. "Now, it's over. We know who you are, we know where you live, we know your name. And in a few minutes, we'll have your fingerprints and your photo in the system, so there'll be nowhere you can hide. Your life as you know it is over. Now that can be a good thing or a bad thing. That's all up to you. All we want is our friends. You help us find them and this ends well. If you don't, you'll be spending the rest of your life in prison, and I'll make sure it's known that you are sexually exploiting children. Prisoners love child molesters. You'll be handed around that prison like the last bar of soap at summer camp. So, what's it going to be? Tell us what we want to know or be the new prison bitch. It's up to you."

"Just tell them!" pleaded Bridgette. "There's no point in not. You don't know who they are."

He eyed her. "And you do?"

"Look at the time. It hasn't even been twenty-four hours since the party and they already found us. This is too big. I know you want out just like I do. This is our chance."

He regarded her for a moment. She was right. He did want out and this was his chance whether he wanted to take it or not, for it *was* over. He sighed. "Fine. I'll tell you everything I know. But then you have to let us go. All of us. Once you hear what I have to say, you'll realize we're just pawns. We're victims too."

One of the women clearly didn't like what he said. "Victim, my ass."

He indicated Cheryl. "She's completely innocent and isn't involved in this at all. She was at the party last night and I found her this morning passed out on the floor like some of them always are, and I brought her home."

"To rape her?"

Cheryl shook her head. "Oh no, he never hurt me. He never even touched me." She stared at him. "But you said you saved me from some guy who had spiked my drink."

Victor shrugged. "Well, your drink *was* spiked, and if I hadn't taken you home with me, somebody far worse might have, someone who's not as much of a gentleman as I am."

The woman rolled her eyes. She clearly had a personal connection to the Americans and didn't have control over her emotions. She could prove dangerous.

Cheryl looked back at her. "I know it's hard to believe, but he really didn't do anything to me. I slept most of the day and then we had dinner and were watching a movie."

The other woman finally spoke. "Do you have any knowledge of what was happening at these parties?"

"No. What *is* happening at the parties?"

"Young men and women like yourself are being kidnapped and sold into sexual slavery." Cheryl's eyes bulged and the woman gestured at him. "And he's involved. He helps run the auction that condemns your friends into a lifetime of rape."

Cheryl's jaw dropped and she stared at him in horror. "Is this true?"

He frowned. "I'm afraid it is, but you have to realize I was like you, living on the streets for years because I was abused by my father. The people I work for found me and offered me a job when they discovered I was good with computers. I didn't realize what I was getting into, but once I was in, there was no getting out." He looked at the man in charge. "Please just let her go. She's got nothing to do with this."

The American glanced at the older one who gave a slight nod.

Perhaps he's *in charge.*

"Fine. When this is all said and done, she can go, but it's time for you to talk."

And he did. He told them everything, from the day he'd been invited to one of the parties, fixed the sound system when it had failed so the party could continue, and was taken aside by someone in charge whom he came to know as the Operator. From that night on, he worked for them, initially just setting up equipment for the raves, then eventually invited into the mobile command center where they ran the auctions out of a converted tour bus. He told them where to find his stash of cash plus his fake IDs, and the calmer woman retrieved them.

"You see, I do want out. I've been planning to get out for months now. Your friends sold for ten million last night. By the end of the week,

I get my 0.2% cut and that gives me enough to get out. If I get my payment on time, I'm gone before the next party."

"Me too," said Bridgette. "That was my plan as well. I've been just waiting for a big payoff. This will be my biggest ever by far. It moved up my timeline by months."

The American turned to her. "And you get 0.2%?"

"No, I only get one." She shrugged. "I guess even in crime, women don't get paid as much as men." She smiled weakly and the calm woman patted her on the shoulder.

"Not the time for jokes, dear."

"Sorry."

The American returned his attention to Victor. "Okay, you've told me your story, but you still haven't told me anything useful. We need to find our friends. How do we do that?"

Victor shook his head. "I don't have any names. The highest person I've ever met is the Operator and I can barely tell you what he looks like."

"Forget names," said the older man, a Brit. "Let's talk method. You drug your victims. Then what?"

"They're taken out of the party, usually by someone like Bridgette, then they're drugged with something a little heavier, sometimes through an injection, sometimes just a drug applied to one of our people's lips. They kiss the goods and they pass out." He raised a hand when he saw the irrational woman was about to explode. "I'm sorry, I shouldn't have said the goods, but you try not to think of them as people, otherwise you realize how vile you've truly become."

"Okay," said the man in charge, apparently the only American in the room. "You drug them, then what?"

"Then they're loaded in the transport."

"What kind of transport?"

"It's a converted semitrailer. It can move twelve at a time."

"And where is this transport?"

Victor shrugged. "I have no idea, but it left at around three this morning, so it's long gone."

"No, I mean, where is it parked when it's being loaded?"

"Oh, very close by. We'll have a secondary access point to the party location, usually one or two alleyways from the party entrance used by the guests. We make sure there's no possibility of cameras catching a shot of the exit point. They're brought up, usually completely unconscious, put into a crate, then wheeled out to the rig which is on the street and then loaded in the back as if it's cargo in case anybody saw us. It's all done very quickly, very efficiently. The truck's only there for maybe ten minutes. Once everyone's loaded inside, the Caretaker transfers them into their pods, and from what I understand, by the time they're outside of Paris, everyone's locked away and the crates are broken down and stowed. This is extremely well financed and well organized. While the operation is taking place, I've heard the Operator on the phone with the people who are clearly his superiors. I've heard different city names mentioned. This has spread around the world."

"And you have no idea who's behind it?"

"None. I know a lot of our bidders are from the Middle East, however, if not most of them."

"How can you be sure?"

"Because they post questions and goad each other on the message board. It's a competition and it's almost always in Arabic."

"How do you know what's being said?"

"The system translates. It's not 100% accurate, but it's close enough to be disgusted by what's being said."

"And the bidder who bought our friends?"

"He's one of our most prolific buyers, HOS-17."

The American regarded him. "HOS-17. Does that stand for anything?"

"Judging from the context and everything I've learned since I've been there, if I had to hazard a guess, House of Saud."

The American cursed as did the older man. "That's going to cause a problem," said the British man.

The American turned to the Brit. "You think this is enough evidence?"

"Oh, it should be enough to get the French police involved, but it's too late for that."

The irrational woman rounded the couch. "What do you mean it's too late?"

"I mean, they're already out of France. The French police should be able to shut down the operation here simply by raiding the next party, but that's it."

She cursed. "I don't care about that." She held up a hand. "Well, obviously I do. You know what I mean. How do we use this to find

Tommy and Mai, how do we get…" She paused. "How do we get our *friends* directly involved."

"We need more evidence that shows more Americans have fallen victim to this."

Victor shifted in his seat. "Well, if you need more evidence, I might be able to help you there."

Unknown Location

Mai rolled onto her back, groaning, her head pounding worse than before. Her rebellion had failed, their captors gassing them, obviously having planned for such an eventuality. She opened her eyes to find a man she didn't recognize standing with a gun pointed at them. She climbed to her knees then woke Tommy, out cold beside her, with a shake, and as the rest slowly woke, zip ties were tossed by the new arrival. She bound Tommy's wrists, and he hers, officially returning them to prisoner status.

The Caretaker woke and sat up, as groggy as the rest of them, also victim to the gas. The new arrival helped him to his feet then cut his bindings with a knife. He handed a gun over and the Caretaker aimed the weapon directly at her and squeezed the trigger without hesitation.

"No!" screamed Tommy, diving in front of her. He cried out as the bullet slammed into his shoulder, spinning him in the air before he collapsed to the ground.

The other arrival smacked the gun down. "Are you insane? Those two are worth ten million!"

The Caretaker spat. "She's probably nine and a half of that."

Mai dropped to the floor, the tears flowing. She rolled Tommy onto his back and he winced. He had taken a round to the right shoulder. The bleeding didn't seem too bad, but she wasn't an expert in these things. She turned on their captors. "He needs a doctor!"

The Caretaker laughed. "All right. You're the doctor. Treat him."

"Do you have a medical kit?"

The other man indicated the cabinet next to her. "Bottom door, right beside you."

She held out her hands. "Cut me loose."

The new arrival stepped forward and sliced the bindings. She tossed the sheet still wrapped around her aside so she could move more freely, then grabbed several bottles of water and the med kit from the cabinet.

"Check if the bullet went through," said one of the other prisoners. She gently lifted Tommy's shoulder off the floor and he gasped. She found a small exit wound, slowly oozing blood.

"It did," she said. "Is that good?"

"Yes, it means we don't have to worry about the bullet doing any more damage inside."

The Caretaker turned to the girl speaking. "How do you know so much about treating bullet wounds?"

"My mother was a nurse. Before she died, she explained a lot of things to me. She wanted me to be a nurse too."

"Am I going to die?" asked Tommy, the fear in his voice heartbreaking, and she didn't know the answer to the question.

"No, you're going to be fine," she lied before setting to work on him with instructions from the girl. While she treated Tommy, everyone else was put back into their pods and the second captor left through a cleverly hidden side door opposite the bathroom. They were soon on their way again, and Mai concluded he must be the driver. He must have had a camera that allowed him to monitor what was going on back here, and it meant there was no hope of escape.

She cleaned and dressed the wound as best she could, but it was clear Tommy needed medical attention sooner rather than later. She turned to the Caretaker. "Please, he needs a doctor."

"I guess you should have thought of that before your little shit-show."

"Please. Just drop him off somewhere so someone can find him. He's not worth anything anymore."

The Caretaker held up his gun. "Then maybe I should just shoot him now."

She draped her body over Tommy. "You'll have to kill me first, and I'm worth too much to you."

The Caretaker chuckled. "You're starting to figure things out." He jutted his chin at Tommy. "If he dies, he dies, and you'll only have yourself to blame. Now shut up or I'll put you back in your pod and *I'll* take care of him."

She squeezed her eyes shut, determined not to cry, but it was no use. The guilt was too much, for he was right.

If Tommy died, it was her fault.

The Château

Paris, France

October 22, 1898

He sat in his chair, a plush affair that was his father's favorite. He had moved it into this private room two months ago to enjoy the parties. To say the extravaganzas he threw were lavish would be an understatement, and from the reaction of the guests, he was quite certain his were the best Paris had ever seen. He was never invited to any of the parties among his peers, thanks to his parents. Torture and kill a few animals out of curiosity and somehow you were branded mentally unstable.

Perhaps he was. How could he know? Either way, he had always been this way and had no desire to change, nor saw any need to. He was content in his own way. He supposed that was happiness, though he had no idea what that emotion truly meant. The only person he ever laughed with was his sister, and she had been labeled as he had been, both of them outcasts kept hidden away from society.

They were each other's only friends, and he was fine with that.

It was ridiculous how they were blamed for their parents' mistake. First cousins shouldn't marry. Everyone apparently knew that, yet they had anyway, and the result was mentally unstable twins. Their parents did something they shouldn't have, and he and his sister were the ones paying the price.

It wasn't fair.

It had been going on for far too long until he put an end to it, until the night his parents had caught him and his sister in bed together. They shouldn't have been surprised. They were, after all, the only members of the opposite sex they were exposed to. Curiosity had won out at a young age, then animal lust had replaced it. It had been going on for years, but they had finally been caught and their parents were furious, threatening to lock them in separate rooms for the rest of their lives.

That's when he had plunged a knife into his father's chest then broke his mother's neck. His sister had merely giggled uncontrollably through the entire ordeal, then suggested the most macabre of ideas as she rubbed her fingers through the blood from her father's wound then spread it on the wall. The idea was shocking, twisted.

Perfect.

Their parents would go away for weeks at a time, abandoning them to the servants. Since they went off to various cities around the world to admire artwork from the greats, it would be a fitting end to insert them into one of the masterpieces they so admired.

There was a knock at the door and he twisted in his chair to see his sister enter. She closed the door and locked it, then strode over seductively, straddling him as she wrapped her arms around his neck and stared down at him.

"Another great party, Brother."

He smiled up at her. "Do you think Mother and Father would be displeased?"

"Oh, they'd be most displeased."

"Good."

She leaned down and gave him a kiss, initiating what had become a ritual at his parties. He never partook, content to stay hidden away, peering through secret peepholes, watching the sons and daughters of society's wealthiest citizens enjoying themselves without a clue as to who was hosting them. It was comforting. It had made him realize he had no desire to be part of that society. They were fools, gluttons, and every one of them deserved whatever fate he might create for them.

At the moment, he was reimagining one of the most famous works by the great one himself, Leonardo da Vinci, his mother's favorite. They needed thirteen to complete the installation, and they already had six. Tonight would be the seventh. His intention had been merely to create the one piece of art in the catacombs underneath the château, but this was proving too much fun, so other masterpieces were being debated, none of which would require so many donations from high society.

He grabbed his sister's hips then one of the bells rattled on the wall beside them, both their heads spinning toward the sound. "Didn't you lock the door?"

"I thought I had. I must have forgotten."

He frowned and she climbed off him. "It looks like business comes first tonight."

Outside Almeria, Spain

Present Day

What a difference twenty-four hours made, especially when the full force of the American government was behind you. Victor had been keeping a record of everyone sold at auction and the information they had on them. He said he hoped he could use it as leverage if he ever got in trouble. There were twelve on the list from the past two years that were identified as American and, according to Leroux, they had already matched them up to missing persons reports, confirming Victor's data. That had been enough for Leroux's boss to authorize the use of CIA resources to investigate the coordinated kidnapping of American citizens and other foreign nationals in an organized human smuggling operation.

Once Leroux's team had been activated in a full CIA operations center with access to their entire bag of tricks, they had quickly found not only the truck used to transport the victims, but the mobile command center used to conduct the auction. The Paris police were now involved, Inspector Fontaine true to her word, opening an investigation the moment she had proof a crime had been committed.

Reading and Humphrey were with the French police as they prepared to take down the Parisian end of the operation, while Spanish police were about to take down the truck before it had a chance to offload its precious cargo. It was critical that the transport be captured smoothly and without incident, the concern being that those involved might kill their victims at the first sign of something going wrong.

The next few minutes were critical.

Interpol Agent Sanchez sat in the passenger seat, her phone pressed to her ear. "Understood." She ended the call and turned back to face Acton and Laura, sitting in the back seat. "The truck is approaching now."

Laura gripped his hand, saying nothing. He leaned forward, peering ahead. An accident had been staged narrowing the road to one lane, police slowly guiding traffic through. A police tactical team was positioned, six hiding behind the concrete barrier on the opposite side of the center divide, another six behind a jack-knifed rig.

The moment they had heard about the operation, Laura had demanded to be there, and Reading had arranged it. They were Interpol observers, and as much as they would both like to be in on the action, there was no way that was happening. He just wished it was Bravo Team here. While he was certain the Spaniards could get the job done, he wasn't as confident that there wouldn't be innocent casualties in the heat of the moment. With Bravo Team, the chances of innocents dying from friendly fire were next to nothing.

"Here they come," said Sanchez. "Black cab, white trailer."

Acton and Laura leaned forward as the semitrailer slowly pulled through the staged accident scene.

"Here it comes."

The police officer guiding the traffic held up his hand and the car in front of the truck came to a stop.

"Please tell me that poor bastard is one of ours," said Acton.

Sanchez confirmed it. "He is."

The truck stopped behind the undercover unit, triggering a flurry of activity. Two tactical team members, one from either side of the vehicle, rushed forward and smashed the driver and passenger side windows of the cab. Two more tossed in flash-bangs as the remainder of the team rose from their hiding positions and opened fire, taking out all the tires.

From his vantage point, Acton couldn't see what was happening behind the truck, but a small explosion erupted as the officers who had taken out the tires stormed the trailer. The doors to the cab were hauled open and the driver yanked out as they all watched, their breaths held, no one saying anything.

Somebody shouted the all-clear and Laura bolted. Sanchez cursed as the car emptied out. Acton chased after Laura with Sanchez behind them, shouting to the Spanish law enforcement officers to let them pass. Laura rounded the end of the trailer first and her anguished cry had him slowing up. Bile filled his mouth as he prepared himself to see Tommy and Mai dead, their young lives snuffed out because he had decided they should go to Paris.

He cursed the money. He cursed the indulgences it provided, for if he was still a poor professor, he never could have afforded to send them on this trip, and they would still be alive. He rounded the end of the trailer and turned to see what Laura was staring at, tears flowing down her cheeks.

And he breathed a sigh of relief.

Nothing.

There was no one there except police.

"What's going on?" he asked in Spanish. "Where are they?"

One of the officers shrugged, pointing at the open doors of twelve pods lining one side of the vehicle. "They're all empty, but it definitely looks like people were in most of them. They must have switched vehicles at some point."

Laura collapsed into his arms and sobbed. "We're too late."

Operations Center 2, CIA Headquarters
Langley, Virginia

Leroux cursed as the entire operations center erupted in frustration with the report that the truck was empty. The door to the room hissed open and their boss, National Clandestine Service Chief Leif Morrison entered the room.

"Did I miss it?" he asked, staring at the screen as he joined Leroux in the center of the room.

"You didn't miss much," muttered Child.

"Why? What happened?"

Leroux explained. "The truck's empty. All we got was the driver."

"Son of a bitch. How's that even possible?"

"Either there was a second truck and we got the wrong one, or they did a handoff at some point."

"But I thought you traced the entire route?"

Leroux shook his head. "No, we *are* tracing it, but we jumped ahead. There's no point in tracing an entire highway when you can assume where it's going and pick it up where there are cameras a few hundred miles down the road." He turned to the room. "Okay, you know what to do. Fill in the gaps. We need to find any place that truck stopped. Start right from the beginning in downtown Paris. Split the route up into manageable chunks, all the way to the takedown. Look for stops, unusual pauses under bridges or bypasses, anything that's out of the ordinary. Sonya, you divvy it up." He smacked his hands together. "Let's get to work, people. It won't be long before they discover we're onto them, and this guy was headed to the south of Spain, which tells me they were going to transport by boat. They might already be on one, and if they are, it's far too easy to toss bodies into the Mediterranean if they think they might be caught."

Tong started shouting off assignments as Morrison stepped closer.

"We've got a problem."

Leroux's eyes narrowed. "What?"

"One of the names on that list the professors acquired is the daughter of a senator."

"Really? It wasn't on the file."

"No, it's been kept hush-hush because there was concern that if whoever took her found out who they had, it could put her in greater jeopardy. It's essential we take prisoners so that we can find out the destinations of these people."

Leroux folded his arms. "Well, sir, the destination is most likely a Middle Eastern country. Saudi Arabia, United Arab Emirates, someplace with oil money. There's no way we'll get them to cooperate. If we're going to do this, we need Delta and we need Washington's support to do whatever it takes."

Morrison smirked. "I had a feeling you were going to say that. The president has already approved the mission. Bravo Team is in Israel, just finishing up a covert op in Syria. They've been seconded to the CIA for the remainder of this mission."

"We're going to need more than a Delta unit if this is turning into a rescue op."

"What do you mean? Our intel says we're looking to rescue ten people."

"Yes, sir. That's this batch. A Black Hawk, maybe a couple of support aircraft will be required, but if we find out the ultimate destinations, we have no idea how many are being held. We could be looking at dozens, if not more."

Morrison chewed his cheek as he thought about the problem. "All right, what are you proposing?"

"If we assume we're going into unfriendly territory, we might have to go in with several Black Hawks or even a couple of Ospreys. They're going to need air cover. Definitely gunships, possibly fighter jets. With mid-air refueling, we can deploy from Italy, or if this is going to be in Saudi, like I think it will, we can go from the USS Nimitz Carrier Strike Group, which is currently in the Arabian Sea."

Morrison sighed. "You're right, but when this goes up in front of the Appropriations Committee for review, I just hope we manage to get the senator's daughter out, otherwise there'll be hell to pay."

Paris Police Prefecture Command Center

Paris, France

Reading and Humphrey stood at the back of the Paris Police Prefecture command center. They were still just observers, despite handing Inspector Fontaine all the evidence she needed. To the woman's credit, she had acted swiftly, and a tremendous amount of resources had been brought online. With help from the CIA, acting as an anonymous source through Reading, they had the location of the modified bus used to run the auctions. But more than that, they had tracked back seven people from the party that Victor identified as all involved, most of them low-level, but one was the Operator, the man who could have all the answers.

Eight teams were spread across the city, ready for a coordinated takedown. He had been standing here for almost an hour, and his legs were shaking. He shifted his weight for the umpteenth time, and Humphrey placed a hand on his arm.

"Are you all right?"

"Just not used to standing for this long anymore."

211

"Me neither. I'll be back in a moment."

She walked over to one of the low-ranking officers in the room and said something, the gofer responding with a crisp nod before leaving the room. She walked over to a table off to the side, returning with two bottles of water. She handed one to him. "Not as good an offering as Sasha's."

He grunted as he unscrewed the cap. "Better than nothing." He took a long swig then smiled when the gofer returned with two chairs. "Merci," said Reading, gratefully dropping into the chair and sighing. Humphrey positioned hers beside him and sat. "Just what an old man needed."

"Bollocks to that old man nonsense. You just have to recover from whatever happened to you in Thailand and you'll be your old self again."

He chuckled. "Maybe one day I'll tell you about it, but I'm not ready to talk just yet."

She stared at him sympathetically. "That bad?"

He nodded as his chest tightened, but said nothing, not trusting his voice.

An order was shouted in the center of the room, the commander of the overall operation giving the go order to all eight teams. Body camera footage erupted into action on the displays filling the front of the room. Reading ignored it all except for one cluster in the center that covered the takedown of the Operator.

He was located in an apartment in a ritzy area, and the RAID team was positioned in the hallway outside. They broke down the door with a battering ram and the team surged inside. All the cameras were on mute, but he could imagine the officers shouting orders to anyone inside. The footage was chaotic, almost useless, but within moments Reading was smiling as a man was led out in handcuffs, one of the cameras catching a clear shot of his face, a face matching earlier surveillance footage that Victor had confirmed was of the Operator.

They had him, and they had him alive. Now, finally, they might get answers.

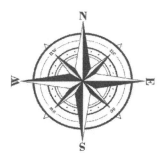

Ramat David Israeli Air Force Base, Israel

"He definitely spit in the man's lap." Sergeant Carl "Niner" Sung held up his phone with the video. "You can see it. Look at his reaction. You don't react like that if you're happy, you react like that when you're looking at your lap and saying, 'WTF, did he just spit on me?'"

Sergeant Leon "Atlas" James sighed, his impossibly deep voice rumbling out a response. "I can't believe you've joined the crowd of idiots that think a celebrity would actually spit on another one at a movie premiere with hundreds of cameras on them. You have to stop getting your news from social media."

Niner eyed him. "So, you're telling me he didn't spit on him?"

"Of course he didn't, just look at the video. Chris Pine is on his phone, in his seat. Then Harry Styles starts walking down the aisle to get to his seat, which is right beside Pine's. Pine puts his phone down between his legs so that he can clap with everyone else to greet his costar. As Styles is sitting down, Pine looks between his legs and stops clapping. Why do you think that is?"

"He's looking for the spit."

"No, you idiot. He's looking at his phone. He obviously got some sort of message. He stopped clapping so that he could see what it said, and by his expression, I'm guessing he didn't like what he saw. But if you keep watching the video, and of course the crazy nutbars who post this garbage don't want you to see it so they cut it out, he resumes clapping, and they're talking and laughing. If you spit in my lap, I'd have belted you. I don't give a shit if I'm on a hundred different cameras, and I'm certainly not going to laugh and joke with you. These dolts who think he spit on him have attention spans shorter than a gnat's. By the time Styles enters the frame, they've already forgotten that Pine was holding a phone."

"Where did it go?"

"Like I said, between his legs, and that's what he's looking at, not a wad of spit."

Niner stared at his best friend then replayed the video. "Huh, what do you know?" He turned to the others in the room. "I think the big man might be right."

Sergeant Will "Spock" Lightman cocked an eyebrow. "You think?"

Niner grinned. "I still believe there's reasonable doubt."

"Then you're an idiot," boomed Atlas.

Sergeant Zach "Wings" Hauser leaned back in his chair and stretched. "Thank God that nonsense is settled. Can we please talk about something other than the latest idiocy from Twitter?"

"I second that," said Sergeant Eugene "Jagger" Thomas. "How about, whose turn it is to host the after-mission barbecue?"

Niner jerked a thumb at Atlas. "I think it's his turn."

Atlas gave him a look. "How the hell can it be my turn? I don't even remember the last time it was your turn."

Niner shrugged. "You must have missed it. Besides, wouldn't everybody here prefer Vanessa's homemade hamburgers than my frozen store-bought ones?"

Hearty agreement from everyone in the room was the response.

Wings leaned forward. "You know how Vanessa loves to entertain and cook. You barely have to lift a finger."

Atlas cocked an eyebrow à la Spock. "Excuse me? After you pigs all go home at the end of the day, I'm the one who cleans up." He wagged a finger. "I'll host, but we do it at the Unit. That way all the garbage just goes in the bins and we walk away clean."

Niner grinned and addressed the team. "Agreed?"

"Agreed!" replied everybody in unison.

Atlas sighed. "Fine. I'll *propose* it to Vanessa when we get home, but I make no promises."

Niner leaned over and squeezed Atlas' shoulder. "Don't worry, big guy. If she gives you any trouble, you have her call me. You know I have a way with the ladies."

The entire room laughed, Niner's track record with women abysmally poor until recently.

"Speaking of Angela, has she dumped you yet?" asked Spock.

"Nope. By some miracle, she seems to think I'm a keeper." Niner cringed as every mouth in the room opened to insult him, then grinned as the commander of Bravo Team, of which they were all members, entered. They were part of America's elite 1st Special Forces Operational Detachment–Delta, commonly referred to by the public as the Delta Force. Command Sergeant Major Burt "Big Dog" Dawson entered with his second-in-command, Master Sergeant Mike "Red" Belme.

"Hey, BD, barbecue at the Unit when we get home. Vanessa's cooking," reported Niner.

Dawson wagged his tablet at them. "Well, tell her to hold off on making any plans. We've got another mission."

Everyone groaned and Sergeant Gerry "Jimmy Olsen" Hudson yawned. "But, BD, we just got off a mission. As much as I love serving my country, I need my beauty sleep."

Spock cocked an eyebrow. "It's way too late for you, dude."

Jimmy gave him the bird.

"This one's personal, gentlemen." Dawson took a seat in the lounge the Israelis had set aside for them to decompress while awaiting transport back home. "We've been seconded to the CIA. They're tracking ten people who were sold at a slave auction in Paris two nights ago. Two are American citizens that we know."

Niner groaned. "Please tell me it's not the docs. Not this time."

"No, but you're close. It's Tommy Granger and Mai Trinh."

All frivolity left the room at the mention of Mai, who had helped save their lives in Vietnam at a great personal cost.

"What's the mission?" asked Atlas.

"We hold for a target location, go in, rescue the hostages and attempt to take as many prisoners as we can for interrogation. Then if we can get a location for where they were headed, we hit it and extract any of the…"

Dawson paused, and it was evident he was struggling. He drew a breath. "Any of the sex slaves we find. These are innocent boys and girls that are being kidnapped from around the world and sold into sexual slavery. Apparently, Tommy and Mai were bought by somebody who might be a member of the House of Saud, the ruling family of Saudi Arabia, and this person bid ten million dollars."

Niner whistled. "Holy shit! If they're paying ten million for the two of them, there's no way they intend to have them mopping floors."

"No, this is absolutely human trafficking with the intention of sexual exploitation. One of the targets we're after at the destination location is the daughter of a US Senator, Chrissy Alberts. She's been missing for over a year, kidnapped in Paris, and her name was on a list of victims supplied to us by a suspect who was arrested earlier."

Atlas held up a finger. "Um, can I ask a stupid question?"

"You always do," muttered Niner.

Atlas shoved him out of his chair and onto the floor.

Dawson waved a hand. "There are no stupid questions."

"I beg to differ," said Niner as he picked himself up. "But let the man speak."

"Why don't we just track Tommy and Mai's group to the final destination?"

"I asked the same question."

Atlas flashed Niner a grin.

"Their suspect-turned-informant said that they don't all go to the same destination. There will be a transfer point where they're split off to be sent to the various bidders. They already hit the truck they thought they were in earlier today, but it was empty. CIA is attempting to find where they were switched out and provide us with a new target. They don't want to risk Tommy and Mai's lives in case there's another switch. The first chance we get to hit them, we're doing so. We'll secure the hostages and hopefully have suspects to interrogate when it's all over." Dawson rose. "Shit, shower, sack. I want everybody rested and ready to go at a moment's notice. Like I said, this one's personal."

Paris Police Headquarters, 1 rue de Lutèce
Paris, France

Reading stood in the corner of the interrogation room, leaning against the wall. Inspector Fontaine, in a delightfully cooperative mood since all eight takedowns had gone smoothly, had agreed to allow him to observe the interrogation of the Operator. Humphrey was behind the glass watching from what was no doubt a comfortable chair, and despite his desire to sit, he remained standing, determined to intimidate their suspect.

Fontaine had been interrogating him for about fifteen minutes and the man was proving uncooperative, instead sitting poker straight in his chair, his hands resting comfortably on the table in front of him, a neutral expression on his face. He gave no indication of being scared or even nervous, despite the evidence they had proving his involvement. The entire interview so far had been conducted in French, and Michelle was translating in his ear.

"CIA says they've cracked the encryption on his phone."

Reading smiled. That was one bit of cooperation he hadn't expected. Fontaine's team had copied the phone's memory and given him a copy for Interpol to use its resources to crack. He had, of course, sent the copy to his Interpol colleagues, but also had sent it to Leroux's team. If they had cracked the encryption, they might have just cracked the case.

He left the room and joined Humphrey in the observation room. "What do we know?"

"Just what I told you." She handed him back his phone. He couldn't turn it off because he was waiting for word from Langley, but he also couldn't bring it in the interrogation as it could prove a distraction even if it were on vibrate.

He turned to one of the others observing. "Is there a private room we could use?"

The woman pointed. "Directly across the hall. It should be empty."

"Thanks." Reading opened the door and Humphrey accepted the chivalry without comment. They crossed into the other room and he dialed Leroux's number, putting it on speaker.

"Agent Reading, I see you got my message."

"I did. What did you find?"

"The motherlode."

Reading exchanged an excited glance with Humphrey.

"It looks like the Operator has kept a record of everything for bookkeeping purposes. He assumed the encryption software he was using would protect it, but unfortunately for him, in his paranoia of keeping his phone off the Internet, he didn't install any of the security upgrades, so we were able to exploit a few little holes that hadn't been plugged on his device."

"And what did you find?"

"Every single transaction that he's been responsible for, going back three years. Unfortunately, a lot of the victims are just given a sequence number because they don't know their names. But others they do and they're filled in, including Tommy and Mai and Senator Alberts' daughter, the dates and times they were put up for auction, the amounts they were sold for, and the handle of the purchaser. From what we can see, HOS-17, who bought Tommy and Mai, also bought the senator's daughter and a lot of the other higher profile names on this list. He seems to be the biggest buyer, but more importantly, from what we can tell, he's the distribution point."

"What do you mean?"

"There are travel itineraries on here that indicate the destination for each batch of victims. The destinations are in code, but many of them match the handles of the bigger purchasers. The working theory is that HOS-17 and several others are the ringleaders, and the victims are transported to a location managed by them, then sent off to the various winning bidders from a country where they don't have to worry about the authorities. Tommy and Mai's group are all slated to be delivered to HOS-17."

"Have you found them yet?"

"Yes, we were able to backtrack to a transfer point outside of Barcelona. A second vehicle took them to the coast where they were loaded onto a boat. That boat already passed its cargo off in Libya where they were just transferred to a private jet."

Reading cursed. "So, there's no chance of intercepting it?"

"No. We could scramble some jets to try to force it down, but they know we won't shoot, so there's no point. Right now, we're better off letting them think they got away with it and see where they ultimately land."

"Where does it look like they're going?"

"We suspect Saudi Arabia, and so far their flight path isn't making me think otherwise."

Reading sat in one of the chairs, arching his back to relieve the tension building all day. "Well, this changes the plan, doesn't it?"

"Absolutely. Bravo Team will no longer be trying to rescue Tommy and Mai's group. Instead, they'll be hitting wherever they end up."

"If they land in Riyadh, are you really going to hit the airport there?"

"No, we'll monitor where they're taken then hit that location. Hopefully we'll find the senator's daughter plus a lot more of the victims."

"If they are going to Saudi Arabia, how long before they land?"

"Four to five hours, depending where."

"Is there any information on his phone about where these other destinations might be?"

"Unfortunately, no, which means we'll probably never find any of the other victims. This is likely a one-shot deal, but at least we'll have shut down part of the network."

"And this buyer, if he is connected to Saudi royalty, what about him?"

"If we extract him, it'll be an international incident. The best we can hope for is that he gets killed in the crossfire."

Reading stared at Humphrey. "Then perhaps crossfire should be encouraged."

Leroux chuckled. "I hear you, sir. I'll see what I can do. Keep everything I told you under your hats. If the French find out, it could leak."

"And Jim and Laura?"

"At your discretion. Just make sure they understand how compartmentalized this is."

"Understood." The call ended and Reading leaned back, folding his arms. "So, what do you think?"

Humphrey sat across from him. "I'm not sure what to think. It's good that they found Tommy and Mai, but we still don't have them yet and any number of things can go wrong. But it's bad in that we might not be able to take down the entire network, which means there are hundreds, maybe thousands of innocent kids out there who will continue to be abused day in and day out."

Reading agreed with her assessment. It was definitely mixed news. But if they could take down the biggest branch of the network and possibly rescue dozens of victims, and if they could eliminate HOS-17, they could protect the lives of hundreds of future victims. He picked up his phone to dial Acton and give him the news. "I say we get Tommy and Mai back, plus the others that are with them, and if we can rescue more, then we're way ahead of where we were yesterday. If we can get an identity on this HOS-17, then even if we can't take him down, we can make sure Langley puts the story out, and perhaps the Saudis will clean up their own house. If we're really lucky, maybe Bravo Team gets a crack at interrogating him and getting some other names."

"Is that the mission, though?"

"It was. They were supposed to take prisoners when rescuing Tommy and Mai so that they could find out their final destination. But now with that part of the plan canceled, I don't know what they're going to do."

"So, what do we do until then?"

"We keep doing our job and hope everyone else does theirs."

Outside Almeria, Spain

Acton hugged Laura, both of them teary-eyed after hearing the update from Reading. Kane's people had located Tommy and Mai, and for now, they had to hope they were still alive and that their friends in Bravo Team would rescue them before their victimization began.

Laura rested her head on his shoulder. "I wish we could be there so they see a friendly face."

He wrapped his arms around her. "They've met most of Bravo Team, and once they're secure, I'm sure they'll be transported to somewhere we can see them quickly enough."

Laura perched on the hood of the Interpol car and her shoulders sagged. "I feel so useless, like we've done almost nothing to help them."

Acton chuckled. "Just because we didn't get to shoot a gun doesn't mean we didn't help our friends. It's because of all the times we've helped before that we have people so willing to help us when we need it. And remember, it was you who caught Bridgette."

"Sasha caught Bridgette."

"You know what I mean. Sasha wouldn't have caught her if you hadn't spotted her and given chase. Because of her, we found Victor. Because of him, we got the evidence we needed to get Leroux's team officially involved. And also because of Victor, we got the Operator, and because of our contacts, Reading was able to pass the data over to the CIA who were able to crack it. So, thanks to all of that, our friends working together, we now have a chance at not only rescuing Tommy and Mai, but saving a whole lot more people. We might have been on the sidelines for a lot of this, but our family wasn't."

She patted his chest. "You're right, of course. I'm just used to being in on the action, I guess."

He laughed. "I think you're forgetting that a lot of times the action we're in on involves a lot of running away."

She snickered. "I suppose you're right. So, what now?"

"Let's reach out to Dylan and make sure he lets us know where they'll take Tommy and Mai after they're rescued. I want to see them the first opportunity we can."

The Château

Paris, France

October 22, 1898

Isabelle's entire body shook with terror. This was stupid, beyond stupid. She had spotted the woman at the end of the hallway go through this very door, a door that lay past a cordon with a sign forbidding anyone from passing. The woman had crossed it without a second thought then unlocked the door with a key fished out of her bustier.

Isabelle had stood for several minutes, debating what to do. The fact the woman had gone through this door with a key meant she wasn't a party guest—she was attached somehow to the household. It had to be the twin sister. It made perfect sense. Twins were inseparable and Jacques' father had said they were both mentally deranged, so much so that they had been hidden away for most of their lives.

Isabelle had made the decision to try the door, certain it would be locked, but it hadn't been, which left her unprepared for what to do now that she found it open. She stood in a spiral staircase, steps leading below and above, the party thudding on the other side of the door as if in the far distance.

She cocked an ear but heard nothing. No footfalls. She had waited too long. If something untoward were happening, she was certain it would be in the lower levels rather than the upper, and as she lifted her foot to take that first step into the basement, she stopped.

What are you doing?

This was insane. She shouldn't be here. This was too dangerous. The girl was here. She either worked here or lived here. She had a key. There was no denying that now. Isabelle had to get back to the others and tell them. She had to find Archambault so the police could get involved.

She turned, reaching for the handle and opened the door, the stairwell she was in flooding with music. She heard something behind her and rather than look, she jammed the whistle in her mouth and blew as hard as she could as someone grabbed her by the scruff of the neck and hauled her back inside, the door slamming shut, her whistle falling silent to those on the other side.

Archambault pointed at Richard. "Go outside and blow your whistle until the police arrive."

Richard stared at him blankly. "What?"

"Do it now!"

Richard bolted for the massive doors open to the night as Archambault sprinted down the corridor to where he was certain he had heard a whistle. Isabelle's friend Sophie had found Richard, and Richard quickly tracked him down. When they couldn't find Isabelle or their suspect, it wasn't too hard to figure out what had happened—Isabelle had ignored his instructions and followed the suspect, most likely down this corridor where he had briefly heard the whistle and saw a door closing at the far end. Angeline and Caroline were on his heels and he waved them back.

"Tell Leblanc where I went!"

They held up and he reached the door, turning the handle, and it opened. He cocked an ear but could hear nothing over the music and the hundreds of excited partygoers. Richard's whistle broke through the din, causing those in the hallway behind him to take notice, the crowds quieting, though the music still blared. Backup would be here soon, but he had to take a chance otherwise Isabelle could be killed.

Someone screamed, the terror-filled exclamation echoing through the stone walls of the stairwell.

Caroline's eyes widened as Guy arrived. "That's Isabelle!"

Archambault pointed at them. "Go get help! Now!"

Guy didn't have to be asked twice as he dashed down the hallway. Archambault pointed at Caroline and Angeline. "Go with him, just to be safe."

Caroline's eyes filled with tears. "You be safe too."

"I will be." He drew his weapon and closed the door, cutting out the sounds of the party, revealing a struggle below. He began down the steps, hugging the outer wall of the spiral stairs, his gun held out in front of him as he advanced toward what, he did not know. The struggle continued, and a man's voice cut through everything.

"Hold her while I get the needle."

230

"I'm trying!" replied a woman.

There was no way they couldn't know he was coming. The music had to have tipped them off when he opened the door, but the struggle had perhaps distracted them enough to not notice. He took each step deliberately, careful not to scrape his foot, careful not to have his footfalls echo. His heart slammed as perspiration beaded on his upper lip and trickled down his back. He had never fired his weapon on the job, and he hadn't even drawn it since working with Leblanc.

This was unfamiliar territory.

A dim light below grew stronger with every step and he readied himself. He had already decided it was too risky to attempt an arrest. Anyone who wasn't Isabelle, he would shoot. He could see the last step below and he braced for what was to come.

"Keep her still! I don't want to jab myself!"

"I've got her, just hurry up."

He stepped onto the floor, the walls surrounding him no longer a smooth stone, but instead the rough surface of the catacombs that ran under much of the old city, the ancient burial grounds of their ancestors. Skulls were embedded in the walls, hundreds of years old, some over a thousand, and it sent a shiver through his body to wonder if any of the missing skulls were now part of the ancient architecture.

He stepped the final few feet into a large room, a long table spread out across the back lit by gas lamps. Six people sat on one side of the table, staring at him, and it took him a moment to realize it was only their heads. Where their bodies should be was nothing, merely the backs of the chairs the heads were mounted to the top of. His stomach churned at the sight.

"Do you have him?" asked a voice from the darkness.

"Yes," replied a woman directly behind him.

Something pierced his neck and he reacted instinctively, realizing that if whoever had injected him pressed down on the plunger, he was dead. He tilted his head toward the needle as opposed to attempting to jerk away, and dropped to a knee while firing his weapon in front of him. All three actions distracted his attacker as he spun around to shoot again, and as he did, something hit him on the side of the head, knocking him to the ground. The gun was yanked from his hand and someone's shoe pressed against his shoulder, flipping him onto his back. A young man and woman stood over him, smiling down at him.

"I think we have our Simon Peter," said the man as he pointed Archambault's gun at him.

The woman cackled, the disturbing utterance echoing through the room. "Yes, he'll do nicely, but I didn't get to have any of my fun."

"There'll be plenty of time for that later. Right now, let's just get that needle in him so he causes us no more trouble."

Operations Center 2, CIA Headquarters

Langley, Virginia

Present Day

The plane had indeed landed in Saudi Arabia, Medina to be exact, and Leroux smiled slightly with the satisfaction that he had been right.

But Morrison cursed beside him. "I should never doubt your gut."

Leroux chuckled. "You'll learn eventually, sir."

Morrison headed for the door. "Keep me posted as to where they end up. I have to let Washington know that this is about to get ugly."

"Good luck."

Morrison left the room as all eyes focused on the satellite imagery displayed on the massive screens arcing across the front of the room.

"Okay, everybody, make sure we're on top of this. Sonya, I want two sets of eyes remaining on that plane even after we think the transfer has happened. They're probably well-practiced at this and may have some method to trick the cameras. I don't want our guys raiding some royal palace and just finding a new construction crew brought in from Libya."

"I'm on it," replied Tong, handing off the assignment to two of the analysts.

Leroux turned to Child. "Any luck getting access to any of the cameras?"

Child shook his head. "No, that section of the airport seems to be a massive blind spot. I can't find any cameras, accessible or otherwise."

Tong grunted. "Gee, that doesn't sound suspicious, now does it?"

Leroux had to agree. A blind spot that size suggested it was intentional, so members of the royal family and the Saudi elite could come and go as they pleased with whomever they pleased. It likely meant smuggling happened here all day, every day. It also meant he was right to suspect cooperation from the Saudis couldn't be counted on, and in all likelihood they would oppose them. "Sonya, let Delta know we've got wheels down. Stand by for final destination."

"On it." She gestured at the screen. "We've got activity."

Leroux returned his attention to the displays to see two black SUVs pull up beside the plane, its door opening and the stairs lowering a moment later. A man stepped out and stood to the side, then people filed out, all wearing matching white outfits.

"Looks more like workers," commented Child.

Leroux had to agree. "Do we have anything at a better angle? Something that might catch one of their faces?"

"No, we've got two satellites on the area, both with top-down views right now. Unless one of them looks up, we won't get anything."

Ten white outfits emerged from the aircraft, one of them helped by two others.

"I think we've got an injury," said Tong then she snapped her fingers as the injured man tossed his head back, likely in pain. "There we go, back it up and get his face!"

Child tapped at his keyboard and a moment later they were all staring at an isolated frame showing an agonized Tommy staring up at the heavens.

"What happened to him?" gasped Tong, one of the few in the room who had met the young man.

Leroux frowned. "I don't know, but he doesn't look good. Relay to Delta that we believe Tommy Granger is injured and may require medical assistance, and *will* require mobility assistance for extraction."

"On it."

"Okay, people, I think we can safely assume that these are our ten victims and a camera blind spot is the extent of their subterfuge. I still want two sets of eyes on that plane just in case there are more people on it." The two SUVs pulled away with their passengers and he pointed at the screen. "All right, this is it. No matter what happens, we can't lose them. If they go into any blind spots, I want eyes remaining on the area, just in case they pull a switch. Work the cameras, try to keep ahead of them."

His phone vibrated with a message and he checked to see it was from Kane.

Diverting to Medina now.

Unknown Location

The hood Mai had been given after getting in the SUV at the airport was yanked off and she squinted at the bright lights before her eyes adjusted. All ten of them were standing inside a building, the design suggesting to her that they were in the Middle East, most likely Saudi Arabia, and whoever owned it was rich. The floors were marble, the columns polished stone, many architectural elements gilded with gold.

The Caretaker faced them, singling out four of the group. "You four head into that room over there." He pointed to a door to the left. "Your new owners will be here to take possession of you shortly. The rest of you, this is your new home until your master tires of you. You will each be paired with a guide who was once like you. They will teach you what is expected, how to groom yourself, how to behave, and what your master's likes and dislikes are. Behave yourself, and who knows? You might just find you like it here."

Mai's stomach flipped at the words. How could anyone like being a slave?

A man in a long flowing robe she would expect to see on the Arabian Peninsula descended a set of nearby stairs, saying nothing, instead standing in front of each of them, looking them up and down. Was this their master, or merely someone who worked for him? He eyed Mai, his face expressionless, then moved on to Tommy, standing beside her. He frowned then tore aside the top of Tommy's jumpsuit, revealing the bandaged shoulder, blood soaking through it.

Something was yelled in what she assumed was Arabic. The Caretaker rushed forward, responding apologetically, though this didn't assuage the new arrival's outrage. The man stormed off and nobody said anything until his footfalls could no longer be heard.

The Caretaker glared at her. "You just cost me two million."

She glared back at him, despite the terror gripping her. "I don't recall firing the shot. You only have yourself to blame."

His nostrils flared and he raised his hand to strike her when she smiled.

"Go ahead and see how many more millions you lose."

He growled in frustration then stepped away, though he didn't take his eyes off her. "I think you're going to prove to be more trouble than you're worth." He clapped his hands twice and half a dozen doors opened to their right, young women appearing in the first five, a young man in the last, all with their hands clasped in front of them, all with their eyes directed to the floor.

All broken.

The Caretaker pointed at Tommy then at the lone young man standing in the doorway. Something was said in Arabic and the young man bowed then stepped toward Tommy, taking him by the hand and leading him toward the door.

Tommy cried, "Mai!" and she reached out for him, tears flowing down her cheeks. He looked back at her, his face weak, his eyes welling, his bottom lip trembling as he struggled to put on a brave face. "I'll be all right. Don't worry about me, just worry about yourself."

The girls emerged from the doorways, taking each of them by the hand, and Mai was led into the room beside where Tommy had been taken. The door closed and she sniffed, wiping her eyes with the back of her hands, finally taking a moment to examine her surroundings. She was in what might be described as a studio apartment with bunkbeds shoved against the wall to the right. There was a small seating area and a door that likely led to a bathroom, though there was no kitchen.

"What happens now?"

The young woman, a blonde Caucasian, gestured at the room. "This will be your home for the next several weeks as you're trained." She pointed to one of the corners where a camera was mounted. "Everything you do and say is monitored. Disobedience won't be tolerated."

"You sound American."

"It's forbidden to talk about our previous lives."

Mai pointed at the wall separating them from where Tommy was. "Will they give my boyfriend proper medical attention?"

"From what the Keeper said, our master paid ten million dollars for the two of you. He's refusing to pay for your boyfriend unless he makes a full recovery. I'm sure he'll be taken care of. Then again, I've seen people killed who are worth far more than two million just because they upset our master. You have to understand, money means nothing to these people, so just because he paid a fortune for you doesn't mean it will protect you." The girl gestured at her. "Take off your clothes so I can see what I'm working with."

Mai folded her arms, rolling her shoulders in. "I'll do no such thing. I am a clean, healthy, properly groomed woman, who's here against her will. That's who you're dealing with."

"Very well, follow me." The woman opened the door and beckoned Mai to come with her. Mai reluctantly followed her down a hallway and around the corner into another corridor, doors lining either side. The woman stopped in front of one of the doors. "What you're about to see is what happens when you don't cooperate."

Her guide opened the door and Mai cried out at the sight before her. A naked woman was mounted, for lack of a better word, to some sort of contraption that had her bent over. Two naked men turned to see who had disturbed them, and her guide bowed, saying something in Arabic. The two men leered at Mai and one of them wagged himself at her.

"You're next." Both returned their attention to the woman who screamed in a language Mai didn't recognize. She squeezed her eyes shut, turning away so as not to see the assault, but there was no avoiding the sounds.

The door clicked shut, silencing the cries.

"Now you see why you have to cooperate? Defiance won't be tolerated. You'll just be handed over to men like that who will abuse you for days on end until you break." The woman's voice lowered. "It's just not worth it. Trust me when I say, it's just not worth it."

239

Mai opened her eyes, wiping them dry. "Did they do this to you?"

"For nine days and then I finally couldn't take it any longer. It just never stopped. You have to understand, you're not a person, you're a piece of meat, you're property, they can do whatever they want to you whenever they want. Complain, that's what happens to you." Her voice cracked, her eyes glistening. "Your life as you know it is over." She led her back toward the room.

"How long have you been here?"

"A little over a year. I resisted, just like you want to, hoping that I would be rescued because of who I was, but they never came, and I realized there was no hope, because if they haven't come to get me by now, then they're never coming."

Mai opened her mouth to ask the obvious question, who was she, but the woman shook her head slightly, her eyes darting toward the camera. It suggested to Mai that her guide was concerned about the camera in the room, but not in the hallways.

The woman closed the door. "Now, take your clothes off."

Mai sighed and reached for the zipper of the jumpsuit she had been given before they were transferred from the semitrailer. She stopped. "My name is Mai, what's yours? Just your first name. Surely there's no harm in that."

The woman's eyes darted toward the camera then she nodded. "I suppose there isn't. You can call me Chrissy."

USS Nimitz
Gulf of Aden

Dawson climbed into the back of the UH-60 Black Hawk, its rotors thundering overhead. The door closed and they lifted off from the deck of the USS Nimitz. Everyone checked their weapons, a mix of Glocks, MP5s, and M4s, with Atlas carrying their shock and awe, the Carl Gustaf 84 mm recoilless rifle that could blast the shit out of a tank if it had to. Dawson activated his comms so everyone could hear and brought up a satellite photo of their destination on his tablet.

"This is the palace of Prince Fahd bin Nayef. He is believed to be HOS-17. He's seventeenth in line for the throne, hence the handle."

Niner elbowed Atlas. "Hence. Dreamy *and* sophisticated."

Dawson continued. "He's got a reputation as a millionaire playboy, likes to spend a lot of time in European capitals drinking and partying, but apparently in his spare time back home, he's purchased himself quite the harem, of which our friends are about to be added. The location is

241

fifteen minutes outside of Medina and isolated, therefore we expect minimal security, and they definitely don't appear to be expecting us."

He pointed at one section of the compound with a building isolated from the main estate. "Our targets are in this building, and unless there's an underground tunnel connecting it to the main structure, which there very well could be, this is where Langley believes they still are. We're going to land right here in the courtyard, fan out, secure the perimeter of this structure, taking out anyone with a gun. We'll make entry, secure the building, then extract any hostages. We'll load them on the Ospreys, evac back to the carrier, all while under the protection of Viper attack helicopters and F-18s flying CAP."

"Easy-peasy, ooh, so breezy," finished Niner. "And what do we do if we've got a little Stockholm Syndrome going on?"

"That's a definite possibility." Dawson pointed at the med kit at Niner's feet. "That's why you've got those sedatives. Anybody who doesn't want to go with us, inject them and we carry them out. If possible, we get some of the other hostages to help. But we don't know how long these people have been there and how indoctrinated they've become. We could find a couple of dozen people desperate to get out, or we could find scores desperate to stay, we don't know. All we do know is that in the long run, they're better coming with us than staying there, no matter how they might feel about it at the moment. Remember, don't let your guard down around the hostages. Even if they appear to be cooperating, any one of them could have been brainwashed and might draw a weapon on you at any time. Assume everyone is hostile. Get them out of the building and onto the Ospreys."

"What about prisoners?" asked Atlas. "Is that no longer part of the plan?"

"No. Washington scrapped that. Most of whom we're dealing with are liable to be Saudi citizens, and the only ones who probably have anything worthwhile to say could all be part of the royal family or their entourage. Washington doesn't want to risk an international incident."

Spock cocked an eyebrow. "And this doesn't?"

"The only reason we're going in is because of Senator Alberts' daughter. The moment we cross into Saudi airspace, the president's calling the Saudis to inform them of the humanitarian operation underway and advising them not to interfere."

"Do you think they'll listen?"

"They will if they know what's good for them, but for now, we go in, take out anyone that's a threat or holding a gun, and bring out the victims. Cleaning up the mess will be left to law enforcement."

Wings spat. "There's no justice for people like that."

"True, but that's not our job today. Today, we're saving Tommy and Mai and whoever else is being held there as slaves for this piece of shit."

Ritz Paris

Paris, France

Acton sat at the table in their hotel suite in Paris, Laura, Reading, Humphrey, and Sasha occupying the other chairs. Langley had informed them that because the other eight hostages were from France, Tommy and Mai would be repatriated along with them if so desired. They had decided it was best rather than joining them somewhere else. The ten victims would have been through one hell of an ordeal together. They would likely have bonded over it and could support each other on the trip back.

Assuming there was a trip back.

Acton's phone vibrated and he brought up the message. "This is it." He tapped the secure link provided by Leroux and put his phone on speaker.

"ETA to target three minutes."

Sasha eyed them. "Just what are we listening to?"

"Live feed of the rescue attempt."

Sasha chuckled. "Archaeology professors, my ass. You're Agency, aren't you?"

Acton gave him a look. "If we were I couldn't tell you, but no, we are archaeology professors who are just extremely well-connected."

"*Zero-One, Control, no evidence that the targets have left the secondary structure. You're cleared to proceed, over.*"

"*Control, Zero-One, acknowledged. Sixty seconds to insertion. Any reaction from the Saudis, over?*"

"*We have four F-16s scrambling out of King Abdullah Air Base. F-18s are en route to intercept and six more have scrambled from the Nimitz. Air superiority will be maintained, which should keep the Saudis at bay. Will advise should they become a problem, over.*"

"*Copy that, Control. We are about to begin insertion. Zero-One, out.*"

Laura gripped Acton's hand tight as they all stared at the phone, each praying in their own way for the safety of all the innocents involved.

Prince Fahd bin Nayef's Palace
Outside Medina, Saudi Arabia

Dawson hopped to the ground, his M4 at the ready as he rushed away from the chopper, his men spreading out behind him. He advanced toward the main entrance of their target structure as two men rushed out through the doors, raising weapons. He put two rounds into each.

He charged toward the entrance to the building, Niner, Atlas, and Spock flanking him as Red led the others around the one-two and one-four corners to secure the perimeter. He glanced up as one of the Vipers fired a rocket, a position near the main palace erupting in a fireball. Gunfire rattled on their six from a distance and Niner cursed.

"Looks like a little more security than we were told."

Dawson glanced toward the palace to see several dozen hostiles rushing out, all brandishing AK-47s and 74s, and he cursed as he activated his comms. "Control, Zero-One. We've got a hell of a lot more activity here than expected. Request you free up the Vipers to even the odds and drop the ROE of minimizing damage to the palace, over."

"Copy that, Zero-One. Stand by," replied Leroux in his ear, and a moment later the shrieking of missiles unleashed from weapons pods filled the air, split-second screams cut off with the deaths of the hostiles.

Dawson reached for the door. There wasn't a moment to lose.

Tommy cried out in agony, a wave of weakness washing over his body as his guide tore the bandage off. Sweat drenched him and his chest heaved with shallow rapid breaths. As he slowly regained focus, he noticed a warmth flowing down his chest. His head lolled to the side and he grew woozy at the sight of blood flowing freely. His idiot guide had clearly torn something, and as the blood pulsed out of him, he grew weaker.

He reached out and grabbed the idiot by the arm. "Please go get my girlfriend."

The young man shook his head. "No, that's not permitted."

"I'm dying." A cloth was pressed into the wound and Tommy winced. "Then tell her I love her, and that I'm sorry I'll never get to see her walk down the aisle on our wedding day."

His guide paused. "You two are engaged?"

Tommy nodded.

"Then I'm sorry. You were never meant to live."

Knots formed in Tommy's stomach. "What do you mean?"

"You were bought so that he could get her. The fact that you were shot just means he can't sell you off. You're now permanently marked as damaged goods. The best you can hope for is to be bought by somebody who either wants to hunt you for sport or slice and dice you. If it were me, I'd be choosing death."

Tears flowed from Tommy's eyes and he reached over, clasping the man's hands pressing into his wound. "Then don't try to save me, just let me bleed out. Just promise me you'll give my fiancée my message."

His guide removed his hands from the wound. "If I can, I will. I promise."

The room vibrated and they both stared up at the ceiling. Tommy immediately recognized it as helicopter rotors, but the fact his guide didn't, and appeared concerned, told him it was an uncommon if not unheard-of occurrence.

He smiled slightly. "They found us."

"What is that?" asked Chrissy.

"A helicopter, I think. Why, don't you guys get helicopters here?"

"Not that I've ever heard." The room shook with an explosion and hope surged through Mai as she grabbed her jumpsuit. Chrissy shrank away from the camera, cowering in the corner. "What's going on?"

Mai grinned. "They've come to rescue us."

Chrissy's jaw dropped. "Oh, no! They'll kill us all!"

Mai zipped up the suit. "What do you mean?" she asked as she slipped on her shoes.

"The Keeper told us once that if anyone tried to rescue us, we'd all be killed."

"How?"

"I don't know."

Mai thought about their experience in the trailer and how they had been gassed. More explosions erupted, violently shaking the room, and suddenly everything went dark. A hissing sound filled her ears and Mai sucked in a deep breath, rushing for the door.

Niner stepped back, turning away from the small charge he had placed on the door. "Fire in the hole!" He flicked the detonator switch and the locking mechanism was destroyed. Dawson rushed forward and hauled the door aside as Atlas and Spock advanced, both firing disciplined rounds as Dawson and Niner followed them in.

"Clear!" announced Spock.

Dawson kicked open the door immediately to his right. He found a darkened room and heard a hissing sound and cursed, yanking the door shut. "Gas! Gas! Gas!" he yelled as he reached for his mask. All four of them quickly fit their gas masks in place and Dawson activated his comms. "Bravo Team, Zero-One. We've got gas inside the building. Take appropriate precautions, over."

Acknowledgments came in over his headset and he opened the door to his right again. He found two young women lying on the floor. He shouldered his weapon and grabbed them both by a hand, dragging them out into the hallway before closing the door. Doors were kicked open up and down the corridor as more of his team entered to cover them, more bodies dragged into the hallway.

"Mai!"

Dawson spun toward Niner's shout as he disappeared into one of the rooms. A moment later, he dragged two figures out and Dawson recognized one of their primary targets, the young woman who had helped save them in Vietnam and sacrificed her future.

"I've got Tommy!" announced Spock as another one was dragged from the room, blood pouring from his shoulder.

Dawson pointed at him. "Niner, take a look."

Niner went to work on Tommy and Dawson pointed at Jimmy. "Start uploading photos of everybody."

"Yes, Sergeant Major."

Explosions outside continued to shake the building, resistance far stiffer than they had anticipated, this slave auction evidently a secret the Kingdom wanted protected.

"Zero-One, Control. The jets the Saudis scrambled have turned back, but we have a substantial ground force that's just left Medina. They're at most fifteen minutes out, over."

Dawson frowned at the lack of specificity. "Define substantial."

"At least two hundred men, including up-armored vehicles, half a dozen of which are equipped with fifty cals."

Gunfire erupted up the stairs ahead and a body tumbled over the railing, smacking the marble floor with a thud. Red's voice came in over the comms.

"Zero-One, Zero-Two. We found something and you're not going to like it, over."

Red slowly shook his head at the sight before him. They had made entry into the building through the rear then pursued two hostiles into the basement. One of the hostiles had triggered something on a security panel just before Dawson's warning about gas came in. Sergeant Donald "Sweets" Peters had been left behind to deal with it as they continued their pursuit, donning their gas masks.

They rounded a corner and the two hostiles they had been chasing sprayed weapons fire at them. Red and Casey hit the floor and returned fire, taking out both men, which was when they noticed the cages. Both sides of the corridor they were in were lined with bars like a prison cell. On the other side were luxurious carpets and pillows and various other accouterments meant for lounging and sleeping, as if conjured from the pages of Arabian Nights.

But that went unnoticed.

Scores of bodies lay sprawled across those carpets and cushions, and he turned back toward where he had left Sweets. "We need that gas shut off, now!"

"Done!" shouted Sweets.

The hissing had already stopped, that fact lost on Red with the horror of what he was looking at. He pointed at the cage doors. "Get those open, blast them if you have to. We need to find out if these people are alive. Sweets, see if you can identify what kind of gas!"

"Stand by! I've uploaded a photo of the canister to Control!"

Sergeant Danny "Casey" Martin blew both cage doors at once and Red rushed inside with the others, taking a knee beside the closest body and pressing his fingertips against the girl's neck. There was a pulse, weak but steady.

His comms squawked. "Bravo Team, Control. We've identified the chemical agent used. It's a knockout gas. I repeat, it's a knockout gas, non-fatal. Keep your masks on, however, as it will take time to dissipate, over."

Red acknowledged the report as did Dawson.

"Zero-One, Zero-Two. We've discovered something here, and you're not going to like it, over."

"Copy that, Zero-Two. Explain, over."

"I'm counting at least fifty, perhaps sixty hostages, all passed out. We're going to need more manpower or a lot more time to get them out, over."

"Copy that, Zero-Two. Begin moving the hostages as best you can, over."

"Roger that, Zero-One. Zero-Two, out." Red turned to the others. "You heard the man. Sweets and Casey, secure the rest of this level, make sure we're alone and cover our sixes. The rest of you, let's start hauling ass. We'll be getting our workout today."

Spock announced the all-clear from the second level and that there were more victims in bed chambers above them. There were so many innocent young men and women here that there was no way it was just for the pleasure of one depraved prince. This was a playground for the Saudi elite, who no doubt treated this as a vacation spot to partake in whatever was on offer. It disgusted him. Dawson would love to get his hands on the guest list and personally terminate every single one of them, but he had a bigger problem. They had anticipated the potential for large numbers, but it had never occurred to anybody that they would all be unconscious and need to be carried, and with a couple of hundred hostiles arriving in less than fifteen minutes, there was no way they could get the job done.

"Zero-One, Control. We've identified the senator's daughter. She was the one with Mai."

Dawson turned back to look. The girl was unrecognizable from the file photo he had seen, but Langley was using facial recognition data points, and if they said it was her then it was her. "Copy that, Control. What's the situation outside, over?"

"Zero-One, the hostiles have been either eliminated or taken cover inside the palace. The pilots report minimal opposition."

"Copy that. Send in the Ospreys. We're beginning this evac now. And tell every able-bodied man on the flight crews to get inside and grab one of our sleeping beauties, over."

"Roger that, Zero-One. Control, out."

Dawson picked up Mai and she groaned, and he hoped that was a sign she would soon be waking up. He jogged toward the front entrance and pushed it open, his M4 leading the way. Outside was chaos. Fires raged and black smoke billowed into the air as the Vipers slowly circled the compound. Their Black Hawk idled nearby as an Osprey swept in, its tilt rotors angling upward as the pilot expertly brought the beast to the ground with a bounce, the rear ramp angled toward Dawson's position. As it slowly lowered, the flight crew rushed out, sprinting toward him as the second Osprey came in for a landing.

Dawson handed Mai over to one of the men. "They're all alive, just unconscious," he said. "They should be coming to soon."

"Yes, Sergeant Major." The man turned around with his precious cargo and headed back to the Osprey. Spock handed the senator's daughter over and Dawson stopped the member of the flight crew.

"We're going to need a stretcher. We've got a wounded man inside."

"I'll bring it back on the next run."

Dawson returned inside with Spock as Red's voice came in over the comms. "This is Zero-Two. We're going to need assistance at the rear of the building. We're bringing out over fifty, all unconscious, over."

Dawson grabbed another of the victims off the floor, slinging the young woman over his shoulder as he headed back out the door. He handed his cargo to a crewmember. "Pack them to the rafters. We might have as many as eighty."

"Holy shit! What the hell's been going on here?"

"I don't even want to think about it. Redirect one of the Osprey's crew to the rear of the building. That's where the majority of them are coming out."

"Yes, Sergeant Major."

Dawson spotted a window of the palace open up and the muzzle of a gun appeared. He aimed his M4 and fired several rounds, eliminating the target. "This is Zero-One, watch the windows. Looks like our hosts are starting to grow some balls again. Zero-One, out."

One of the Vipers sprayed the facade of the building with its cannons, scarring the showpiece to Saudi wealth, hopefully making anyone inside think twice about engaging. One of the flight crew ran past with a stretcher and Dawson followed him inside. The crewman helped Niner load Tommy onto it and they were soon outside. Dawson grabbed the last of the victims they had discovered on the first floor then redirected the others to the second floor. He handed over the girl and surveyed the area.

"Control, Zero-One. What's the status of that column, over?"

"ETA eight minutes," was the reply. "We have four more Vipers and two more Black Hawks inbound, along with six F-18s. ETA five minutes. If they want it, we're going to give them one hell of a fight, over."

Dawson cursed. He had no doubt they would win any fight against the Saudis with that kind of air power. The problem was the lucky shot. The Ospreys used for the evacuation were lumbering beasts, as were the Black Hawks. A lucky shot could kill half of those they were rescuing.

"Control, we need to think outside of the box. I need a pilot with balls for a special mission."

Over the Rescue Site, Saudi Arabia

Major Chariya "Apocalypta" Em grinned as she activated her comms. "CAG, this is Apocalypta, I'd like to volunteer for that mission, over."

The CAG chuckled. "I thought you might. No one has bigger balls than you."

"Permission to proceed?"

"Granted."

"Copy that, CAG. Eagle Zero-Three inbound. ETA two minutes." She banked hard to starboard then leveled out, pushing forward on the throttle, the F-18E Super Hornet rapidly gaining speed as she adjusted her course to the new target now loaded in her system. She began her descent, picking up even more speed as the distance between her and the Saudi column approaching the rescue site quickly closed.

The mission was insane, but those were the kind she loved. The Saudis were supposed to be their allies, sort of, so Washington didn't want any direct engagement with their forces beyond those at what was apparently a horrendous crime scene. She had been listening to the chatter, and it sounded like at least sixty innocent young girls and boys had been found, and the only way to get them out safely was to buy more time.

And that was now her job.

She spotted the column below and banked slightly, aligning with the road the Saudis were on. She roared up behind them, faster than the speed of sound, and blasted over them no more than twenty feet above their heads. She cut her speed, banking hard to port and coming back for a second pass. As she made her turn, she got a good view of the column and laughed. The Saudis had scattered in a panic, the entire column brought to a halt.

"This is Eagle Zero-Three. Looks like our Saudi friends are going to need a few minutes to regroup and change their diapers. I'll continue to monitor just in case they need another demonstration of just what this baby can do, over."

The CAG's voice cut in. "Good job, Apocalypta. I think you scared the living shit out of them. Hopefully they'll be taking their time as they change their shorts. Keep a safe distance. CAG, out."

Apocalypta gained some altitude, continuing in a slow circle over the column and smiled.

I love my job.

Prince Fahd bin Nayef's Palace
Outside Medina, Saudi Arabia

Dawson breathed a sigh of relief as the Osprey lifted off with the first load of their rescued victims, including Tommy, Mai, and the senator's daughter Chrissy. One of the Vipers sprayed a volley in front of the palace, reminding anyone inside that dared fire on the departing aircraft just what was in store for them. Two F-18E escorts circled overhead, then as the Osprey gained speed, settled in on either side.

The second Osprey taxied closer to the rear of the building and Dawson jogged over to the Black Hawk that had brought them in. He climbed on board and leaned closer to the pilot. "Sir, as soon as that second Osprey has taken off, reposition to the rear of the building. We'll load on as many of the survivors as you can fit, and you get them back to the carrier."

"And what about you guys?"

"There's another Black Hawk inbound. We'll take it. The most important thing is getting these kids to safety."

"So, it's true? This was some sort of sex slave brothel?"

Dawson nodded. "It's quite the horror show. You wouldn't believe some of the things we found in there."

"Like what?" asked the young copilot.

"Trust me, you don't want to know." Dawson disembarked and headed for the rear of the building, some of the flight crew from the first Osprey remaining behind, adding to the manpower carrying what by Red's count were fifty-six victims from the basement.

"Zero-One, Control. Osprey One has cleared Saudi airspace, over."

Dawson smiled at Leroux's update. If he died here today, he'd die well, knowing he had saved thirty-two innocents.

But the job was nowhere near done.

Ritz Paris

Paris, France

Acton couldn't remember the last time he had been so tense. His empty water bottle remained gripped in his hand, the plastic crushed, the fact going unnoticed as they all huddled around his phone, listening to the feed from Langley.

"Control, Zero-One. Can someone let the professors know that Tommy and Mai have successfully made it out of Saudi airspace, over?"

"Zero-One, Control. They're monitoring. Professors, if you didn't catch that, Tommy and Mai are on board the first Osprey heading for the USS Nimitz and are now in international airspace."

Laura cried out in relief and Acton's grip relaxed, the plastic crackling as they both embraced each other. Reading and Humphrey shook hands and Sasha rounded the table, giving everyone a high five, as caught up in the moment as any of them.

"Oh, thank God!" cried Laura. "I don't think I've been so scared in my life."

Acton agreed. "They're safe, but this isn't over. BD and his men are still in there and so are, by the sounds of it, another forty or fifty victims."

"God, I hope they can get the rest of them out safely."

Reading grunted. "If anyone can do it, it's Bravo Team."

Humphrey exhaled loudly. "What I don't understand is why are the Saudis resisting? They've been told what this is all about."

"I can only think of two reasons. Either they're doing it because it's a violation of their territory and any one of our countries would do the same, or they know full well what's going on there and are trying to protect their dirty little secret. Remember, after today, there's no way they can deny anything, and I have no doubt that every country with the capability will be reviewing their satellite footage of that palace and figuring out just who visited it. When this hits the press, I have no doubt there are going to be a lot of Jeffrey Epsteins in this world sweating a little heavier."

"I hope so," said Laura. "And I hope every one of them ends up swinging from the end of a rope."

"Command, this is Osprey One. Notify the med deck that our patient just stopped breathing. Resuscitation efforts underway, over."

Acton's entire body weakened as Laura collapsed into his arms. "Was anyone else injured?" he asked the room, a question he already knew the answer to.

Reading frowned. "No, I don't believe so."

Acton held on to Laura, both of them squeezing each other tight. "It's all my fault."

Over International Airspace

"Tommy!" screamed Mai as the heart monitor hooked up to her fiancé flatlined. She rushed to his side but was pushed back by the medic working on him. Chrissy grabbed her and held her tight as everyone fell silent, all attention now on the life and death struggle taking place before their very eyes. The man she loved had sacrificed himself to save her, and right now, she'd rather be dead than be the one who survived this ordeal.

She squeezed her eyes shut, burying her head in Chrissy's shoulder as the medic placed the defibrillator pads in position. The whine of the machine charging was torture and she begged God to save the sweetest man she had ever met.

"Clear!" shouted the medic, his warning rapidly followed by a sickening zap then thump, the monitor beeping then resuming its steady final tone. "Charging!"

This was all her fault. He had jumped in front of a bullet meant for her, a bullet that never would have been fired if she hadn't instigated their escape attempt. If she had just given in like the others and cooperated, the rescue by Bravo Team would have still happened and they would both be on this plane alive and well.

Oh God, I'm so sorry! Please tell him, I'm so sorry!

The defibrillator zapped the love of her life again and again, the flat tone of death resuming each time.

Prince Fahd bin Nayef's Palace
Outside Medina, Saudi Arabia

Dawson covered the front windows of the palace as the second Osprey, fully loaded, lifted off, a warning volley from one of the gunships again signaling to any remaining hostiles that they should let it go unmolested. It slowly rose off the ground then the rotors tilted forward and it picked up momentum, the F-18s circling overhead taking up position on its wings, ready to take the hit should a missile be launched. The Black Hawk at the front of the building lifted off, slowly banking around to the rear where the last half-dozen victims remained.

Dawson turned to the others. "The moment it touches down, everybody on board!"

Gunfire erupted from the palace and Dawson, along with Atlas and Spock, sprinted under the chopper, placing themselves between it and the palace, opening fire, Atlas firing the half-dozen rounds from the recoilless rifle, destroying what remained of the facade of the once magnificent palace.

"Zero-One, Control. That column is sixty seconds out, over."

Dawson glanced over his shoulder to see the Black Hawk touching down, the rest of his team and the aircrew that had remained behind from the Ospreys hauling their barely conscious cargo toward its open doors.

"Zero-One, Control. Osprey Two has cleared Saudi airspace."

Dawson took a brief moment to smile then resumed his suppression fire at the building as two of the Vipers did the same far more effectively.

"BD!"

Dawson glanced over his shoulder to see Niner beckoning them. Dawson rose. "Everybody in the chopper!"

Atlas and Spock turned and sprinted toward the Black Hawk as Dawson fell back, covering them with continued fire. They were about to be at their most vulnerable. Gunfire erupted from behind him and he spun to see the Saudi column arriving at the front gates.

"Control to Vipers. You're clear to engage the arriving column, over."

The attack helicopters providing cover banked hard, pulling 180s as Dawson turned and sprinted toward the chopper. He dove inside, somebody grabbing him by the belt and hauling him in the rest of the way as the Black Hawk lifted off. The doors were slammed shut and bullets pinged off the fuselage. He climbed to his feet then peered out one of the windows to see the Vipers open fire, the buzz of their cannons accompanied by screeches from their missile pods welcome, but the end result even more so.

Saudi vehicles erupted in explosions, instantly killing those inside or standing nearby, the few survivors scattering as those manning the

Vipers showed no mercy, just like the victims held here had been shown none. This was retribution. This was revenge. This was justice that would never be delivered by the system, and he just wished he was behind the controls, incinerating those who would commit such atrocities for their own pleasure.

This entire kingdom deserved to burn to the ground.

The Black Hawk tilted forward slightly then they gained speed, rapidly leaving the palace grounds behind. The Vipers broke off their attack and joined them, covering their exfil.

An alarm sounded in the cockpit.

"Missile lock!. We've got incoming!" warned the copilot.

"Brace for impact!" shouted Dawson, everyone grabbing on to whatever they could find. He watched out the window as one of the Vipers banked away from them, the contrail of a missile screaming toward them from one of the survivors on the ground. The attack helicopter opened up, its cannons roaring in a desperate attempt to shoot down the missile as the Black Hawk and its escorts deployed countermeasures. The missile continued toward them unabated as they banked away, the thumping of the deploying chaff and flares vibrating the airframe.

An explosion ripped through the air behind them and Dawson closed his eyes in silent prayer for the crew that had heroically sacrificed themselves for their comrades-in-arms and the innocent ghosts forgotten by society but not the brave men and women who had put their lives on the line today to do the right thing.

He just prayed justice would be delivered.

Outside Prince Fahd bin Nayef's Palace

Outside Medina, Saudi Arabia

Kane peered through the scope of his M24 Sniper Weapon System, supplied to him by a contact shortly after arriving in Medina on tickets paid for by the professors. This wasn't an official op. This was payback. He was about half a mile from the smoldering wreck that once had been the palace of a Saudi prince. The devastation his scope revealed was satisfying. At least half of the column that had arrived was dead, most of the other half wounded, and very few security personnel from the palace grounds appeared to have survived, most emerging from the palace dressed as servants.

A man in the robes of a sheik emerged from the front entrance and Kane focused on him. "Confirm with Control that this is the target."

They weren't on official comms, instead, this mission run through his secure network. Sherrie had her phone pressed to her ear. "Control, confirm that's our target." She gave a thumbs-up. "Target confirmed. Man in white robes at top of steps."

267

Kane took aim then drew a breath as he moved his finger from the trigger guard to the trigger, then gently exhaled as he squeezed. The target dropped and he took a moment to confirm the vermin wasn't moving, then scrambled back to the other side of the dune they had been perched atop. They hopped on their dirt bikes and headed for the coast, where if all went according to plan, a Zodiac was waiting to retrieve them.

Justice, at least partially, delivered.

The Château

Paris, France

October 22, 1898

Leblanc and his men rushed through the entrance, Richard leading the way toward a hallway just to the left. He had over fifty men with him, all waiting for Archambault's signal, the vast majority of them down the hill. He and one officer in plain clothes had been in a carriage out front, pretending to deal with a broken wheel.

He spotted Guy and Caroline beckoning him. "Hurry!" she cried as the crowds parted.

He pointed at the other officer. "Kill that music!"

The officer nodded, looking about for the source as Leblanc sprinted down the hallway.

"There's a door at the far end!" shouted Guy. "He went through there!"

269

Leblanc reached the door and yanked it open as he drew his weapon, praying his foolish young partner hadn't turned himself into the fifth victim.

Isabelle lay huddled against the wall, her head throbbing from where she had been struck, her entire body aching from the manhandling she had received as she was shoved down the stairs and into what she was discovering was a chamber of horrors. Archambault was dead. She was sure of it. After the man had hit him in the head and knocked him out, the woman had injected him with something. The two of them were now struggling to get him in one of the empty chairs at the table, the woman giggling the entire time, the man more serious, though clearly enjoying himself judging by the odd smile on his face. Archambault was propped up in the chair then a clamp was tightened around the bottom of his neck.

They both stood back and the man smiled. "There we go, picture perfect."

The woman noticed they had an audience and she grinned at her. "Don't worry, my dear, there's plenty of room at the table for you."

The man stepped back and turned toward Isabelle, holding out a hand toward the table. "So, what do you think of my reinterpretation of Da Vinci's Last Supper?"

Isabelle stared at him for a moment, confused, and she tore her eyes away from his and took in the scene before her. Da Vinci's Last Supper? Then she recognized it. The long table, all the guests on one side, with only the heads to represent Jesus and the apostles, including at the far left where Bartholomew would have sat, the head of her beloved Jacques.

She screamed.

The woman screamed as well, mimicking her, which merely added to the terror of the moment. Isabelle struggled to her feet but her knee buckled in agony and she collapsed.

"Go get another injection for her."

"Another woman in your recreation of Jesus and his male apostles? Wasn't Mother enough?"

The man shrugged as Isabelle realized these were indeed the twins spoken of. "When the flesh has rotted off their heads, they'll all look alike. Remember, Sister, that these are creations for the ages." He suddenly stopped and cocked an ear. "Something's wrong."

His sister turned toward the stairs. "What?"

"The music has stopped. Did you lock that door?"

"No, we were too busy with her."

"Go lock it quickly!"

The sister darted toward the stairwell when a gunshot rang out, stopping her in place before she crumpled to the ground. Leblanc rushed into the room, aiming his weapon at the brother.

"Oh, thank God!" cried Isabelle. Leblanc made brief eye contact with her before he finally realized what he was looking at.

"Daniel!" he cried as he spotted Archambault fastened to the chair. He aimed his weapon directly at the brother. "Is he still alive?"

"He was dead the moment he dared interfere with my work."

"Your work?"

The brother extended a hand toward his horrific creation. "Don't you recognize it? Da Vinci's Last Supper? Your friend here, Daniel, did you say his name was? He makes a fine Simon Peter, doesn't he? A police officer taking the place of the apostle that attempted to defend Jesus from arrest. I think it's a fitting tribute to your friend's memory, don't you? To be immortalized like this for eternity?"

Leblanc stared at him. "You're sick! What the hell are you talking about? Why would you do such a thing?"

The brother gestured at two of the heads where Jesus and John would have sat. "Don't you recognize my mother and father? Two of Parisian society's most renowned patrons of the arts, who've made it a point to abandon their children throughout their lifetimes in order to visit the works of the great artists renowned throughout history. Now *they* are the art, part of my masterpiece. Mother and Father will rest in peace for eternity, in the catacombs that have long preserved our past." He smiled at Leblanc as he stepped over to one of the chairs and placed his hands on the back of it. "I think you would make a fine Judas, don't you?"

"I think you're under arrest."

The man smiled, holding out his wrists. "Then please, arrest me."

Leblanc stepped forward and Isabelle gasped as the floor opened up in front of him. He dropped with a cry, but not before he threw his gun toward her and disappeared out of sight, his shout cut short with the sickening sound of blades piercing flesh.

Her captor quickly rounded the table as Isabelle reached for the gun. She grabbed it and twisted onto her back, raising it as he closed in on her. She closed her eyes as she squeezed the trigger, the recoil shocking.

He gasped and she opened her eyes to find him still coming toward her, blood trickling down his chest. She fired again, then again, each time his body jerking from the impact as he still came at her, his strides now mere shuffles.

She fired twice more and he finally collapsed to his knees then fell to his side, his eyes pure evil, piercing her soul as he glared at her.

"You'll pay for what you've done to the Grangier family."

Landstuhl Regional Medical Center

Landstuhl, Germany

Present Day

Tommy woke to unfamiliar sounds. As he cut through the fog, he recognized machines beeping, fans whirring, and announcements over a PA system. He must be in a hospital. He forced his eyes open and spotted somebody standing over his bed.

"Hey, sleepyhead, about time you woke up."

Tommy smiled, the figure still out of focus but the voice unmistakable. "Professor Acton, what happened?"

"You were shot. Then you died. Welcome to the club."

Tommy chuckled. "Am I going to live?"

"Oh, you'll be fine." Acton pressed a straw against Tommy's lips and he took a sip then several more. "There's something I need to tell you though, and it might come as a bit of a shock, but don't worry, you're going to be okay."

Tommy tensed, the heart rate monitor ticking up a few beats per minute.

"What? What's happened?"

"They were able to revive you, but you slipped into a coma and you're just now waking from it."

"Oh my God, how long was I out?"

"This is the tough part. It's been twelve years."

Tommy gasped, pushing up on his elbows. He winced and glanced down to see his shoulder still bandaged. "Wait a minute. If it's been twelve years, why haven't I healed?"

Acton laughed as the door to the hospital room opened and Mai and Laura stepped in. His prankster turned to them. "He figured it out in like five seconds."

Laura gave him a stern look. "Don't tell me you played that trick on the poor boy."

"I had to. How often do you get an opportunity to do something like that?"

Mai rushed forward, hugging Tommy. "Thank God you're all right."

He kissed her hand then gripped it to his chest. "Will somebody please tell me what's really going on? Was I in a coma?"

Laura patted his cheek. "Yes, you were, my dear. Twelve days."

"So not twelve years?"

"No. My husband's an asshole. You should know that."

Tommy gave the still grinning Acton a look. "I'm beginning to realize that."

Acton shrugged. "One day, when I'm lying in a hospital bed dying, I give you permission to pull the plug."

Tommy quickly extended a hand. "Deal."

Acton roared with laughter and shook his hand. Tommy lay back down, his shoulder still aching. "So, what *did* happen? I remember getting shot, I remember my guide doing something that caused it to bleed even more, and then I remember hearing a hissing sound and passing out. After that, it's a complete blank."

The door opened again and Reading entered. "Ah. You're finally awake. It's about bloody time."

"Hello, sir."

"How are you feeling?"

"Fine. A little confused."

Laura turned to Reading. "My asshole husband told Tommy he had been in a coma for twelve years."

Reading laughed and high-fived Acton. "I can't believe you had the bollocks to do it."

"You owe me twenty bucks."

Laura eyed them both. "You mean this was a bet?"

Acton shrugged. "Between gentlemen."

Laura rolled her eyes. "I don't see any gentlemen in this room except for Tommy."

Tommy held up his hands. "Will somebody *please* tell this gentleman what happened?"

Acton perched on the side of the bed. "Well, from what I've been told by Leroux, when Bravo Team hit the palace grounds, your captors

276

triggered a fail-safe and gassed all the prisoners to knock them out so they wouldn't be a problem. Bravo Team managed to disable the gas, then carried you all out of the building, and you were evacuated by two Ospreys and a Black Hawk."

"How many?"

"Almost eighty."

"Did anybody get hurt?"

"You mean besides you?"

Tommy nodded.

"One helicopter crew sacrificed themselves, taking a missile hit in order to save everybody on the Black Hawk including Bravo Team."

Tommy closed his eyes and thanked them with a silent prayer. "And those who kidnapped us, what happened to them?"

"The French police arrested the entire crew operating out of Paris," said Reading, stepping closer to the bed. "Interpol is coordinating to locate other cells. More importantly, however, now that we know who was behind it, half a dozen different governments are examining satellite footage to identify anybody who ever visited the prince. And we're already getting a lot of names."

"Like whom?"

Reading shook his head. "Sorry, I can't say. But if charges are filed, you'll read about it in the press because there'll be no keeping this secret unless deals are struck."

Acton patted Tommy on the leg. "But you'll be happy to know that the prince behind this is dead. Mutual friends took him out shortly after you were evacuated."

Tommy smiled. "Good." He clasped Mai's hand. "And you're all right? Nothing happened to you?"

She kissed his hand, holding it against her lips. "I'm fine. Nothing happened, thank God. Bravo Team got there just in time."

Tommy turned to Acton. "Make sure you pass on my thanks to them."

"I will. When Mai told the guys what you did for her, Dawson said it was a ballsy move, but he recommended that next time you do it with a vest."

Tommy laughed then winced. "Well, at least I wasn't naked."

"Huh?"

Mai giggled. "I guess I forgot to mention they had us all naked until we left the semitrailer."

Acton frowned. "I'm sorry to hear that." He slapped Tommy's leg. "Good thing they didn't take me hostage."

"Why's that?"

"Because if you saw me naked, you'd feel inadequate for the rest of your life."

Laura groaned and Mai snickered as Reading turned his back on his friend, shaking his head. Tommy simply smiled, giving Acton the finger. He turned to Mai. "At least I know I'm not dead."

"How's that?"

"Because I think I've led a good enough life to get into Heaven, and the jokes have to be better there than they are here."

Acton returned the bird. "Okay, fine, wiseass. If you don't like my jokes, then maybe you'll like my history lesson. How about I tell you how the wealthy Grangier family of Paris fled their home after an unspeakable scandal, and became the Granger family we know and love today?"

THE END

ACKNOWLEDGMENTS

This one was a lot of fun to write. The James Acton Thrillers series, and its spinoffs, now span 56 novels, and have a rich set of characters that have become family. One of the reasons I enjoyed this one is that other characters were given a chance to shine. Tommy and Mai, especially Mai, featured prominently, we got to see Reading in action again, and of course Kane and Leroux's team doing what they do best—getting Bravo Team into position.

A James Acton Thriller is no longer just James Acton—it's the friends and family he and Laura have built up over the years, which is the way I've written most of my books. Perhaps it comes from watching a lot of ensemble cast movies and shows.

When the preorder for this book launched, later that day it was announced that Queen Elizabeth II had died. Sales immediately slowed for the rest of the day, indicating that this was a story that even those outside the Commonwealth were interested in.

I saw the Queen and her husband, Prince Philip, when they last visited Ottawa in 2010. I would have shaken her hand but thousands of people were in my way, so, alas, all I caught was a few glimpses of them both. It was a cool experience, and I was surprised at being caught up in the excitement as I'm not an avid royal watcher.

With her death, I now feel privileged to have seen her in person.

As usual, there are people to thank. My dad for all the research, Brent Richards for some weapons info, the real Chris Leroux for some French help, Ian Davidson for some motorcycle info, and, as always, my wife, my daughter, my late mother who will always be an angel on my shoulder as I write, as well as my friends for their continued support, and my fantastic proofreading team!

To those who have not already done so, please visit my website at www.jrobertkennedy.com, then sign up for the Insider's Club to be notified of new book releases. Your email address will never be shared or sold.

Thank you once again for reading.

Made in the USA
Columbia, SC
09 May 2023

16246705R00174